"OH, MY SOUL, IT'S COMING! DON'T GO OUT THERE!"

It was there, Lythande could feel it waiting, circling, prowling, its hunger a vast evil maw to be filled. She knew it hungered for her, to take in her body, her soul, her magic. If she spoke, she might find herself in its power.

It was coming; the Blue Star between her brows was prickling like live coals, the blue light burning through her brain from the inside out. As it loomed over her, shadowing the whole of the innyard, she clenched her hand on the rough wooden handle of the kitchen hag's knife and thrust up into the greater darkness that was the Walker.

She was not sure whether the scream that enveloped the world was her own scream of terror, or whether it came from the vast dark vortex that swirled around the Walker. She only knew she was caught in a monstrous whirlwind that swept her off her feet into darkness, dampness and horror. . . .

—from *The Walker Behind*

MERCEDES LACKEY
in DAW editions:

Spell Singers

(Original title: Bardic Voices One)

by
Marion Zimmer Bradley
Mercedes Lackey
Jennifer Roberson
Ru Emerson

Edited by Alan Bard Newcomer

DAW BOOKS, INC.
DONALD A. WOLLHEIM, PUBLISHER

DAW Book Collectors No. 765.

First DAW Printing, December, 1988

2 3 4 5 6 7 8 9

PRINTED IN CANADA
COVER PRINTED IN U.S.A.

Contents

Introduction

There are writers everywhere. They pour out pages and pages of how-to-articles, newspaper reports, advertising copy and introductions to books.

And, of course, there are people who write stories, lots of writers, lots of stories, some of each both good and bad. Writing is a craft and many stories are written by competent craftspeople, and we enjoy them. But there is a very special breed of writer out in the world.

This special breed is the storyteller. They manage to work into their writing the special magic that has descended down from the great oral tradition of storytelling. They are the spell singers of our modern age—the literal and lineal descendants of the harpers, minstrels, troubadours and bards.

The how-to-writer is basically a teacher, and the reporter is the equivalent of the old town crier. Storytellers had to hold their listeners spellbound with their words; if they didn't, then they probably didn't eat. They took the old themes of good and evil and rewove older stories into new tales.

The minstrel might sing a song, then pause

(dramatically, of course), "Let me tell you a story. A *strange* thing happened in Windhill Town last week, I heard this from old Maggie, who says *she* saw it happen."

Listeners might throw another log on the fire, fill a glass, find a more comfortable spot; then they all leaned in closer, so as not to miss a word.

Nowadays we have it easier, we just buy a book. Then we set the thermostat at seventy degrees, heat some coffee in the microwave, open the book and sit down and read.

Now you can put that book down whenever you want, you don't have to listen closely to catch every word. But these stories are special, by special people who make you want to catch every word. The writers in this book are storytellers, singers of words on paper, they gather you in and then pause (grammatically, of course), "Let me tell you a story . . ."

So let me throw another log on the fire, I got this story from . . . it's about the strange things that happened in . . . last week, so just make yourself comfortable, pull up your book and listen.

Alan Bard Newcomer
Eugene, Oregon
March 1988

10

Balance

by Mercedes Lackey

You're my bodyguard?"

The swordsman standing in the door to Martis'
cluttered quarters blinked in startled surprise.
He'd been warned that the sorceress was not easy
to work with, but he hadn't expected her to be
quite so rude.

He tried not to stare at the tall, disheveled mage
who stood, hands on hips, amid the wreckage
she'd made of her own quarters. The woman's
square features, made harsher by nervous tension, reflected her impatience as the mercenary
groped for the proper response to make.

Martis was a little embarrassed by her own ill
manners, but really, this—child—must surely be
aware that his appearance was hardly likely to
evoke any confidence in his fighting ability!

For one thing, he was slim and undersized; he
didn't even boast the inches Martis had. For another, the way he dressed was absurd; almost as
if he were a dancer got up as a swordsman for
some theatrical production. He was too clean, too
fastidious; that costume wasn't even the least worn-
looking—and silk, for Kevreth's sake! Blue-green

11

silk at that! He carried two swords, and whoever had heard of anyone able to use two swords at once outside of a legend? His light brown hair was worn longer than any other fighter Martis had ever seen—too long, Martis thought with disapproval, and likely to get in the way despite the headband he wore to keep it out of his eyes. He even moved more like a dancer than a fighter.

This was supposed to guard her back? It looked more like she'd be guarding *him*. It was difficult to imagine anything that looked less like a warrior.

"The Guard-serjant did send this one for that purpose, Mage-lady, but since this one does not please, he shall return that another may be assigned."

Before Martis could say anything to stop him, he had whirled about and vanished from the doorway without a sound. Martis sighed in exasperation and turned back to her packing. At this moment in time she was not about to start worrying about the tender feelings of a hire-sword!

She hadn't gotten much farther along when she was interrupted again—this time by a bestial roar from the bottom of the stair.

"MARTIS!"

The walls shook with each step as Trebenth, Guard-serjant to the Mage's Guild, climbed the staircase to Martis' rooms. Most floors and stairs in the Guild-hold shook when Trebenth was about. He was anything but fat—but compared to the lean mages he worked for, he was just so—massive. Outside of the Guards' quarters, most of the Guild-hold wasn't designed to cope with his bulk. Martis could hear him rumbling under his breath as he ascended; the far-off mutterings of a volcano soon to erupt. She flinched and steeled herself for the inevitable outburst.

He practically filled the doorframe; as he glared at Martis, she half expected steam to shoot from his nostrils. It didn't help that he *looked* like a volcano, dressed in Mage-hireling red, from his tunic to his boots. The red of his uniform matched the red of his hair and beard, and the angry flush suffusing his features.

"Martis, what in the name of the Seven is your *problem?*"

"My *problem*, as you call it, is the fact that I need a bodyguard, not a temple dancer!" Martis matched him glare for glare, her flat gray eyes mirroring his impatience. "What are you trying to push on me, Ben? Zaila's toenails, if it weren't for the fact that Guild law prevents a mage from carrying weapons, I'd take sword myself rather than trust my safety to *that* toy!"

"Dammit, Martis, you've complained about every guard I've ever assigned to you! *This* one was too sullen, *that* one was too talkative, *t'other* one *snored* at night—" he snorted contemptuously. "Mother of the Gods, Martis, *snored?*"

"You ought to know by now that a mage needs undisturbed sleep more than food—besides, anyone stalking us would have been able to locate our campsite by ear alone!" she replied, pushing a lock of blonde hair—just beginning to show signs of gray—out of her eyes. The gesture showed both her annoyance and her impatience; and pulling her robe a bit straighter could not conceal the fact that her hands trembled a little.

Trebenth lost a portion of his exasperation; after all, he and Martis were old friends, and she *did* have a point. "Look, when have I ever sent you a guard that couldn't do the job? I think this time I've really found the perfect match for you—he's quiet, half the time you don't even know he's there, in fact—and Mart, the lad's *good*."

"*Him?* Ben, have you lost what little mind you ever had? Who told you he was good?"

"Nobody," he replied, affronted. "I don't take anyone's word on the guards I hire. I tested him myself. The boy moves so fast he doesn't *need* armor, and as for those two toy swords of his, well—he's good. He came within a hair of taking *me* down."

Martis raised an eyebrow in surprise. To her certain knowledge, it had been years since anyone could boast of taking Trebenth down—or even coming close. "Why's he dress himself up like a friggin' faggot, then?"

"*I* don't know, Mart. Ask him yourself. I don't care if my guards wear battle-plate or paint themselves green, so long as they can do the job. Mart, what's bothering you? You're not usually so damn picky. You generally save your complaining till the job's over."

Martis collapsed tiredly into a chair, shoving aside a box of tagged herbs and a pile of wrinkled clothing. Trebenth saw with sudden concern the lines of worry crossing her forehead and her puffy, bruised-looking eyelids. "It's the job. Guild business—internal problems."

"Somebody need disciplining?"

"Worse. Gone renegade—and he's raising power with blood-magic. He was very good before he started this; I've no doubt he's gotten better. If we can't do something about him now, we'll have another Sable Mage-King on our hands."

Trebenth whistled through his teeth. "A black

adept in the making, eh? No wonder they're sending you."

Martis sighed. "Just when I'd begun to think the Guild would never set me to anything but teaching again. But that's not what's troubling me, old friend. I knew him—a long and close association. He was one of my best students."

Trebenth winced. To set Martis out after one of her old students was a cruel thing to do. The powers manipulated by mages gifted them with much that lesser folk could envy—but those powers took as well as gave. Use of magic for any length of time rendered the user sterile. In many ways Martis' students took the place of the children she'd never have.

They often took the place of friends, too. She'd served the Guild since she'd attained Masterclass, and her barely past what for the unTalented would have been marriageable age. There were few sorcerers among her contemporaries, male or female, that didn't secretly envy and fear the Masterclass mages. There were no mages of her own rank interested in taking a lover whose powers equaled their own. They preferred their women pliant, pretty, and not too bright. Martis' relations with her own kind were cordial, but barren.

Trebenth himself had been one of the few lovers she'd had—and she hadn't taken another since he'd toppled like a felled tree for his little Margwynwy, and she'd severed that side of their relationship herself. It was at times like this one, with her loneliness standing bare in her eyes, that he pitied her with all his heart.

Martis caught his glance, and smiled thinly. "The Council did their level best to spare me this, I'll give them that much. The fact is, we don't know for certain how deeply he's gotten himself in yet; we know he's been sacrificing animals, but so far rumors of *human* deaths are just that—rumors. They want to give him every chance to get himself out of the hole he's digging for himself. Frankly, he's got too much Talent to waste. One of the factors in deciding to send me is that they hope he'll give me a chance to reason with him. If reason doesn't work, well, I'm one of the few sorcerers around with a chance of defeating him. After all, I taught him. I know all his strengths and weaknesses."

"*Knew*," Trebenth reminded her. "Can I assign Lyran to your service, now that I've vouched for his ability, or are you still wanting someone else?"

"Who? Oh—the boy. All right, Ben, you know what you're doing. You've been hiring guards as long as I've been training mages. Tell him to get the horses ready, I want to make a start before noon."

When Martis had finished ransacking her room for what she wanted, she slung her packed saddlebags over her shoulder and slammed the door on the entire mess. By the time she returned—*if* she returned—the Guild servants would have put everything back in order again. That was one of the few benefits of being a Masterclass sorceress. The Guild provided comfortable, safe quarters and reliable servants who never complained—at least not to her. Those benefits were paid for, though; a Masterclass mage lived and died in service to the Guild. No one with that rating was ever permitted to take service independently.

Martis had a liking for heights and a peculiar phobia about having people live above her, so her room was at the top of the staircase that linked all four floors of the Masters' quarters. As she descended the stairs, she found that a certain reluctant curiosity was beginning to emerge concerning this unlikely swordsman, Lyran. The order she'd given Trebenth, to have the lad ready the horses, was in itself a test. Martis' personal saddlebeast was an irascible bay gelding of indeterminate age and vile temper, the possesser of a number of bad habits. He'd been the cause of several grooms ending in the Healer's hands before this. Martis kept him for two reasons—the first was that his gait was as sweet as his temper was foul; the second that he could be trusted to carry a babe safely through Hell once it was securely in the saddle. To Martis, as to any other mage, these traits far outweighed any other considerations. If this Lyran could handle old Tosspot, there was definitely hope for him.

It was Martis' turn to blink in surprise when she emerged into the dusty, sunlit courtyard. Waiting for her was the swordsman, the reins of his own beast in one hand and of Tosspot in his other. Tosspot was not trying to bite, kick, or otherwise mutilate either the young man or his horse. His saddle was in place, and Martis could tell by his disgruntled expression that he hadn't managed to get away with his usual trick of "blowing" so that his saddle girth would be loose. More amazing still, the swordsman didn't appear to be damaged in any way, didn't even seem out of breath.

"Did he give you any trouble?" she asked, fastening her saddlebags to Tosspot's harness, and adroitly avoiding his attempt to step on her foot.

"He is troublesome, yes, Mage-lady, but this one has dealt with a troublesome beast before," Lyran replied seriously. At just that moment the swordsman's dust-brown mare lashed out with a wicked hoof, which the young man dodged with reflexive agility. He reached up and seized one of the mare's ears and twisted it once, hard. The mare immediately resumed her good behavior. "Sometimes it would seem that the best animals are also the vilest of temper," he continued as though he hadn't been interrupted. "It then is of regrettable necessity to prove, that though they are stronger, this one has more knowledge."

Martis mounted Tosspot, and nodded with satisfaction when his girth proved to be as tight as it looked. "I don't think this old boy will be giving you any more trouble. From the sour look he's wearing, I'd say he learned his lesson quite thoroughly."

The swordsman seemed to glide into his saddle and gracefully inclined his head in thanks for the compliment. "Truly he must have more intelligence than Jesalis," he replied, reining in his mare so that the sorceress could take the lead, "for this one must prove the truth of the lesson to her at least once a day."

"Jesalis?" Martis asked incredulously; for the jesalis was a fragile blossom of rare perfume, and nothing about the ugly little mare could remind anyone of a flower.

"Balance, Mage-lady," Lyran replied, so earnestly that Martis had to hide a smile. "So foul a temper has she, that it is necessary to give her a sweet name to leaven her nature."

They rode out of the Guild hold in single file with Martis riding in the lead, since protocol demanded that the "hireling" ride behind the "mistress" while they were inside the town wall. Once they'd passed the gates, they reversed position. Lyran would lead the way as well as providing a guard, for all of Martis' attention must be taken up by her preparations to meet with her wayward former student. Tosspot would obey his training and follow wherever the rider of Jesalis led.

This was the reason that Tosspot's gait and reliability were worth more than gold pieces. Most of Martis' time in the saddle would be spent in a trancelike state as she gradually gathered power to her. It was this ability to garner and store power that made her a Masterclass sorceress—for after all, the most elaborate spell is useless without the power to set it in motion.

There were many ways to accumulate power. Martis' was to gather the little aimless threads of it given off by living creatures in their daily lives. Normally this went unused, gradually dissipating, like dye poured into a river. Martis could take these little tag-ends of energy, spin them out and weave them into a fabric that was totally unlike what they had been before. This required total concentration, and there was no room in her calculations for mistake.

Martis was grateful that Lyran was neither sullen nor inclined to chatter. She was able to sink into her magic-gathering trance undistracted by babble and undisturbed by a muddy, surly aura riding in front of her. Perhaps Ben had been right after all. The boy was so unobtrusive that she might have been riding alone. She spared one scant moment to regret faintly that she would not be able to enjoy the beauties of the summer woods and meadows they were to ride through. It was so seldom that she came this way . . .

The atmosphere was so peaceful that it wasn't until she sensed—more than felt—the touch of the bodyguard's hand on her leg that she roused up again. The sun was westering and before her was a small clearing, with Lyran's horse contentedly grazing and a small, neat camp already set up. Martis' tent was to the west of the clearing, a cluster of boulders behind it, and the tent-flap open to the cheerful fire. Lyran's bedroll lay on the opposite side. Jesalis was unsaddled, and her tack laid beside the bedroll. From what Martis could see, all of her own belongings had been placed unopened just inside the tent. And all had been accomplished without Martis being even remotely aware of it.

"Your pardon, Mage-lady," Lyran said apologetically, "but your horse must be unsaddled."

"And you can't do that with me still sitting on him." Martis finished for him, highly amused. "Why didn't you wake me earlier? I'm perfectly capable of helping make camp."

"The Guard-serjant made it plain to this one that you must be allowed to work your magics without distraction. Will you come down?"

"Just one moment—" There was something subtly wrong, but Martis couldn't pinpoint what it was. Before she could say anything, however, Lyran seized her wrist and pulled her down from her saddle—just as an arrow arced through the air where she had been. Lyran gave a shrill whistle and Jesalis threw up her head, sniffed the breeze, and charged into the trees to their left. Martis quickly sought cover in some nearby bushes, as Lyran threw himself to the ground and rolled up into a wary crouch.

A scream from where the mare had vanished indicated that the horse had disposed of the archer, but he had not been alone. From under the cover of the trees stepped not one, but three swordsmen.

Lyran regained his feet in one swift motion, drew the swords he wore slung across his back, and faced them in a stance that was not of any fighting style Martis recognized. He placed himself so that they would have to pass him to reach her.

The first of the assassins—Martis was reasonably sure that this was what they were—laughed and swatted at Lyran with the flat of his blade in a careless, backhanded stroke, aiming negligently, for his head.

"This little butterfly is mine—we will see if he likes to play the woman he apes—" he began.

Lyran moved, lithe as a ferret. The speaker stared stupidly at the sword blade impaling his chest. Lyran had ducked and come up inside his guard, taking him out before he'd even begun to realize what the bodyguard was about.

Lyran pulled his blade free of the new-made corpse while the assassin still stood. He whirled to face the other two before the first fell to the ground.

They moved in on him with far more caution than had their companion, circling him warily to attack him from opposite sides. He fended off their assault easily, his two swords blurring—they moved so fast—his movement dancelike. But despite his skill, it seemed he could not find an opening to make a counterattack. For the moment all three were deadlocked. Martis chafed angrily at her feeling of helplessness; the combative magics she'd prepared were all meant for use against another mage. To use any of the spells she knew that worked against a fighter, she'd have to reach her supplies in her saddlebags—now rather hopelessly out of reach. She noted that she was sharply aware of the incongruous scent of the crushed blossoms that lay beneath the dead man's body.

The deadlock was broken before Martis could do more than curse at her own helplessness. Within the space of a breath, Lyran feinted at the third of the assassins, drawing the second to attack. He caught his opponent's blade in a bind, and disarmed him with practiced ease. Then the other lunged at him, and he moved aside just enough for his blade to skim past his chest. Lyran's left-hand blade licked out and cut his throat—with the recovery of the stroke that had disarmed the other. Before Martis could blink, Lyran continued the flow of movement so swiftly that before the one could fall, the sword in his right hand had cut the remaining assailant nearly in half.

And behind him, the first dead man rose, sword in hand, and hacked savagely at the unsuspecting Lyran's blind side. Lyran got one blade up in time to defeat the blow, but the power behind it forced him to one knee. The Undead hammered at the bodyguard, showing sorcerous strength that far exceeded his abilities in life. Lyran was forced down and back, until the Undead managed to penetrate his defenses with an under-and-over strike at his left arm. The slice cut Lyran's arm and shoulder nearly to the bone. The sword dropped from his fingers and he tried to fend off the liche with the right alone. The Undead continued to press the attack, its blows coming even faster than before. Lyran was sent sprawling helplessly when it caught him across the temple with the flat of its blade.

Martis could see—almost as if time had slowed—that he would be unable to deflect the liche's next strike.

She, Lyran, and the Undead all made their moves simultaneously.

Martis destroyed the magic that animated the corpse, but not before it had made a two-handed stab at the bodyguard.

But Lyran had managed another of those ferret-quick squirms. As the liche struck, he threw himself sideways—a move Martis would have thought impossible—and wound up avoiding impalement by inches. The Undead collapsed then, as the magic supporting it dissolved.

Freed from having to defend himself, Lyran dropped his second blade, groped for the wound, and sagged to his knees in pain.

Martis sprinted from out of hiding, reaching the swordsman's side in five long strides. Given the amount of damage done his arm, it was Lyran's good fortune that his charge was Masterclass! In her mind she was gathering up the strands of power she'd accumulated during the day, and reweaving them into a spell of healing; a spell she knew so well she needed nothing but her memory to create.

Even in that short period of time, Lyran had

had the presence of mind to tear off the headband that had kept his long hair out of his eyes and tie it tightly about his upper arm, slowing the bleeding. As Martis reached for the wounded arm, Lyran tried feebly to push her away.

"There is—no need—Mage-lady," he gasped, his eyes pouring tears of pain.

Martis muttered an obscenity and cast the spell. "No guard in *my* service stays wounded," she growled, "I don't care what or who you've served before; I take care of my own."

Having said her say and worked her magics, she went to look at the bodies while the spell did its work.

What she found was very interesting indeed, so interesting that at first she didn't notice that Lyran had come to stand beside her where she knelt. When she did notice, it was with some surprise that she saw the slightly greenish cast to the guard's face, and realized that Lyran was striving valiantly not to be sick. Lyran must have seen her surprise written clear in her expression, for he said almost defensively, "This one makes his living by the sword, Mage-lady, but it does not follow that he enjoys viewing the consequences of his labor."

Martis made a noncommittal sound and rose. "Well, you needn't think your scoutcraft's at fault, young man. These men—the archer, too, I'd judge—were brought here by magic just a few moments before they attacked us. I wish you could have taken one alive. He could have told us a lot."

"It is this one's humble opinion that one need not look far for the author of the attack," Lyran said, looking askance at Martis.

"Oh, no doubt it's Kelven's work, all right. He knows what my aura looks like well enough to track me from a distance and pinpoint my location with very little trouble, and I'm sure he knows that it's me the Guild would send after him. And he knows the nearest Gatepoint, and that I'd be heading there. No, what I wish I knew were the orders he gave this bunch. Were they to kill—or to disable and capture?" She dusted her hands, aware that the sun was almost gone and the air was cooling. "Well, I'm no necromancer, so the knowledge is gone beyond my retrieval."

"Shall this one remove them?" Lyran still looked a little sick.

"No, the healing-spell I set on you isn't done yet, and I don't want you tearing that wound open again. Go take care of Tosspot and find your mare, wherever she's gotten herself to. I'll get rid of them."

Martis piled the bodies together and burned them to ash with mage-fire. It was a bit of a waste of power, but the energy liberated by the deaths of the assassins would more than make up for the loss—though Martis felt just a little guilty at using that power. Violent death always released a great deal of energy—it was a shortcut to gaining vast quantities of it—which was why blood-magic was proscribed by the Guild. Making use of what was released when you had to kill in self-defense was one thing—cold-blooded killing to gain power was something else.

When Martis returned to the campsite, she discovered that not only had Lyran located his mare and unharnessed and tethered Tosspot, but that he'd made dinner as well. Browning over the pocket-sized fire was a brace of rabbits.

"Two?" she asked quizzically. "I can't eat more than half of one. And where did you get them?"

"This one has modest skill with a sling, and there were many opportunities as we rode," Lyran replied. "And the second one is for breakfast in the morning."

Lyran had placed Tosspot's saddle on the opposite side of the fire from his own, just in front of the open tent. Martis settled herself on her saddle to enjoy her dinner. The night air was pleasantly cool, night creatures made sounds around them that were reassuring because it meant that no one was disturbing them. The insects of the daylight hours were gone, those of the night had not yet appeared. And the contradictions in her guard's appearance and behavior made a pleasant puzzle to mull over.

"I give up," she said at last, breaking the silence between them, silence that had been punctuated by the crackle of the fire. "You are the strangest guard I have ever had."

Lyran looked up, and the fire revealed his enigmatic expression. He had eaten his half of the rabbit, but had done so as if it were a duty rather than a pleasure. He still looked a bit sickly.

"Why does this one seem strange to you, Magelady?"

"You dress like a dancer playing at being a warrior, you fight like a friggin' guard-troupe all by yourself—then you get sick afterward because you killed someone. You wear silks that would do a harlot proud, but you ride a mare that's a damn trained killer. What *are* you, boy? What land spawned something like you?"

"This one comes from far—a great distance to

the west and south. It is not likely that you have ever heard of the People, Mage-lady. The Guard-serjant had not. As for why this one is the way he is—this one follows a Way."

"*The* Way?"

"No, Mage-lady. *A* Way. The People believe that there are many such Ways, and ours is of no more merit than any other. Our way is the Way of Balance."

"You said something about 'balance' before—" Now Martis' curiosity was truly aroused. "Just what does this Way entail?"

"It is simplicity. One must strive to achieve Balance in all things in one's life. This one—is on a kind of pilgrimage to find such Balance, to find a place where this one may fit within the pattern of All. Because this one's nature is such that he does well to live by the sword, he must strive to counter this by using that sword in the service of peace—and to cultivate peace in other aspects of his life. And in part, it must be admitted that this one fosters a helpless outer aspect," Lyran smiled wryly. "The Mage-lady will agree that appearing ineffectual does much to throw the opponent off his guard. So—that is the *what* of this one. As to the *why*—the People believe that the better one achieves Balance, the better one will be reborn."

"I certainly hope you don't include good and evil in your Balance—if so, I'll do the cooking from now on."

Lyran laughed. "No, Mage-lady, for how could one weigh 'good' and 'evil'? Assuredly, it was 'good' that this one slew your foes, but was it not 'evil' to them? Sometimes things are plainly one or the other, but too often it depends upon where one stands one's own self. A primary tenet of our Way is to do no harm when at all possible—to wound, rather than kill, subdue rather than wound, reason rather than subdue, and recall when reasoning that the other may have the right of it."

"Simple to state, but—"

"Ai, difficult to live by. It would seem that most things worth having are wrapped in difficulty. Have you not spent your life in magecraft, and yet still learn? And does this not set you farther apart from others—sacrificing knowledge for the common ties of life?"

Martis scrutinized her companion across the flames. Not so young, after all. Not nearly so young as she had thought—nor so simple. It was only the slight build, the guileless eyes, the innocence of the heart-shaped face that made you think "child." And attractive too. Damned attractive. . . .

Don't be a fool, she scolded herself. *You haven't the time or energy to waste—besides, he's young enough to be your son. Well, maybe not your son. But too damned young for the likes of you! Hellfires! You have more to think about than a sweet-faced hireling! Get your mind back to business.*

"Before we sleep, I'm intending to gather power as I was doing on the road," she stretched a little. "I want you to rouse me when the moon rises."

"Mage-lady—would quiet chanting disturb you?" Lyran asked anxiously. "This one would offer words for those slain."

"Whatever for? They wouldn't have mourned *you!*" Once again, Lyran had surprised her.

"That is their Way, not this one's. If one does not mourn that one has slain, the heart soon dies. Under other circumstances, might they not have been comrades?"

"I suppose you're right," Martis replied thought-fully. "No, chanting isn't going to disturb me any. Just make sure you also keep a good watch out for any more surprises."

"Of a certainty, Mage-lady," Lyran didn't even seem annoyed at the needless admonition, a fact that made Martis even more thoughtful. Professional mercenaries she'd known in the past tended to get a bit touchy about mages giving them "orders" like she'd just given him. Nothing much seemed to ruffle that serene exterior. How long, she wondered, had it taken him to achieve that kind of mind-set? And what kind of discipline had produced it? A puzzle; truly a puzzle.

The next day brought them to a ring of standing stones—the Gate-site. The inherent magic residing in this place made it possible to use it as a kind of bridge to almost any other place on the earth's surface. Martis had been to Kelven's tower once, and with mage-habit had memorized the lay of the land surrounding it. They would be able to ride straight from *here* to *there* once the proper spell was set into motion. This would have another benefit, besides saving them a long and tiring journey; Kelven would "lose" them if he had been tracking them, and without knowing exactly where to look for them, would not know how many of them had survived his attack. They rested undisturbed that evening, with Martis quickly regaining from the place the energy she spent in shielding their presence there.

The Gate spell took the better part of the next morning to set up. Martis had no intentions of bringing them in very near, for she had other notions as to how she wanted this confrontation to be played out. After a light noon meal, she activated the Gate.

The standing stones began to glow, not from within, but as if an unquenchable fire burned along their surfaces. The fire from each reached out to join with the fires of the stones on either side. Before an hour had passed, the ring was a near-solid thing of pulsating orange light.

Martis waited until the power-flux built to an internal drawing that was well-nigh unendurable —then she led the two of them at a gallop between two of the stones. They rode in through one side— but not out the other.

They emerged in the vicinity of Kelven's tower— and the confrontation Martis had been dreading was at hand.

She wasn't sure whether the fact that there had been no attempt to block them at the Gate was good or bad. It could be that Kelven was having second thoughts about the situation, and would be ready to be persuaded to amend his ways. It also could be that he was taking no further chances on the skills of underlings or working at a distance, and was planning to eliminate her himself in a sorcerers' duel.

They rode through country that was fairly wild and heavily wooded, but Kelven's tower lay beyond where the woods ended, at the edge of a grass-plain. Martis described the situation to Lyran, who listened attentively, then fell silent. Martis was not inclined to break that silence, lost in her own contemplations.

"Mage-lady—" Lyran broke into Martis' thoughts not long before they were to reach Kelven's stronghold. "—is it possible that the Mage-lord may not know about the continued survival of this one?"

"It's more than possible, it's likely," Martis told him. "I've been shielding our movements ever since the attack."

"But would you have gone on if this one had fallen? Would it not have been more likely that you would return to the Guild Hall to seek other guards?"

They had stopped on the crest of a ridge. Below them lay grasslands and scrub forest that stretched for furlongs in all directions but the one they had come. Kelven's tower was easily seen from here, and about an hour's distance away. The sun beat down on their heads, and insects droned lazily. The scene seemed ridiculously incongruous as a site of imminent conflict.

Martis laughed—a sound that held no trace of humor. "Anybody else but me *would* do just that. But I'm stubborn, and I've got a rotten temper. Kelven knows that. He watched me drag myself and two pupils—he was one of them—through a stinking, bug-infested bog once, with no guides and no bodyguards. The guides had been killed and the guards were in no shape to follow us, y'see; we'd been attacked by a Nightmare. I was by-Zaila not going to let it get away back to its Lair! By the time we found it, I was so mad that I fried the entire herd at the Lair by myself. If you'd been killed back there, I'd be out for blood—or at least a *damn* convincing show of repentance. And I wouldn't let a little thing like having no other guard stand in my way."

"Then let this one propose a plan, Mage-lady. The land below is much like this one's homeland. It would be possible to slip away from you and make one's way hidden in the tall grass—and this one has another weapon than a sling." From his saddlebag Lyran took a small, but obviously strong bow, unstrung, and a quiverful of short arrows. "The weapon is too powerful to use for hunting, Mage-lady, unless one were hunting larger creatures than rabbits and birds. This one could remain within bowshot, but unknown to the Mage-lord, if you wished."

"I'm glad you thought of that, and I think it's more than a good idea," Martis said, gazing at the tower. Several new thoughts had occurred to her, none of them pleasant. It was entirely possible that Kelven wanted her here, had allowed them to walk into a trap. "If nothing else—this is an order. If Kelven takes me captive—shoot *me*. Shoot to kill. Get him too, if you can, but make sure you kill me. There are too many ways he could use me, and anyone can be broken, if the mage has time enough. I can bind my own death-energy before he can use it—I think."

Lyran nodded, and slipped off his mare. He rearranged saddle-pad and pack to make it appear that Martis was using the ill-tempered beast as a pack animal. In the time it took for Martis to gather up the mare's reins, he had vanished into the grassland without a trace.

Martis rode toward the tower as slowly as she could, giving Lyran plenty of time to keep up with the horses and still remain hidden.

She could see as she came closer to the tower that there was at least one uncertainty that was out of the way. She'd not have to call challenge to bring Kelven out of this tower—he was already waiting for her. Perhaps, she thought with a brightening of hope, this meant he *was* willing to cooperate.

When Lyran saw, after taking cover in a stand of scrub, that the mage Kelven had come out of his tower to wait for Martis, he lost no time in getting himself positioned within bowshot. He actually beat the sorceress' arrival by several moments. The spot he'd chosen, beneath a bush just at the edge of the mowed area that surrounded the tower, was ideal in all respects but one—since it was upwind of where the mage stood, he would be unable to hear them speak. He only hoped he'd be able to read the mage's intentions from his actions.

There were small things to alert a watcher to the intent of a mage to attack—provided the onlooker knew exactly what to look for. Before leaving, Trebenth had briefed him carefully on the signs to watch for warning of an attack by magic without proper challenge being issued. Lyran only hoped that his own eyes and instincts would be quick enough.

"Greetings, Martis," Kelven said evenly, his voice giving no clue as to his mind-set.

Martis was a little uneasy to see that he'd taken to dressing in stark, unrelieved black. The Kelven she remembered had taken an innocent pleasure in dressing like a peacock. For the rest, he didn't look much different from when he'd been her student—he'd grown a beard and mustache, whose black hue did not quite match his dark brown hair. His narrow face still reminded her of a hawk's, with sharp eyes that missed nothing. She looked closer at him, and was alarmed to see that his pupils were dilated such that there was very little to be seen of the brown irises. Drugs sometimes produced that effect—particularly the drugs associated with blood-magic.

"Greetings, Kelven. The tales we hear of you are not good these days," she said carefully, dismounting and approaching him, trying to look stern and angry.

"Tales. Yes, those old women on the Council are fond of tales. I gather they've sent you to bring the erring sheep back into the fold?" he said. She couldn't tell if he was sneering.

"Kelven, the course you're set on can do no one any good," she faltered a little, a recollection of Kelven seated contentedly at her feet suddenly springing to mind. He'd been so like a son—this new Kelven *must* be some kind of aberration! "Please—you were a good student; one of my best. There must be a lot of good in you still, and you have the potential to reach Masterclass if you put your mind to it." She was uncomfortably aware that she was pleading, and an odd corner of her mind noted the buzzing drone of the insects in the grass behind her. "I was very fond of you, you know I was—I'll speak for you, if you want. You can 'come back to the fold,' as you put it, with no one to hold the past against you. But you must also know that no matter how far you go, there's only one end for a practitioner of blood-magic. And you must know that if I can't persuade you, I have to stop you."

There was a coldness about him that made her recoil a little from him—the ice of one who had divorced himself from humankind. She found herself longing to see just a hint of the old Kelven; one tiny glimpse to prove he wasn't as far gone as she feared he must be. But it seemed no such remnant existed.

"Really?" he smiled. "I never would have guessed."

Any weapon of magic she would have been prepared for. The last thing she ever would have expected was the dagger in his hand. She stared at the flash of light off the steel as he lifted it, too dumbfounded to do more than raise her hands against it in an ineffectual attempt at defense.

His attack was completed before she'd done more than register the fact that he was making it.

"First you have to beat me, *teacher*," he said viciously as he took the single step between them and plunged it into her breast.

She staggered back from the shock and pain, all breath and thought driven from her.

"I'm no match for you in a sorcerer's duel—" he said, a cruel smile curving his lips as his hands moved in the spell to steal her dying power from her. "—not yet—but I'll be the match of *any* of you with all I shall gain from your death!"

Incredibly, he had moved like a striking snake, his every movement preplanned—all this had taken place in the space of a few eyeblinks. She crumpled to the ground with a gasp of agony, both hands clutching ineffectually at the hilt.The pain and shock ripped away her ability to think, even to set into motion the spell she'd set to lock her dying energy away from his use. Blood trickled hotly between her fingers, as her throat closed against the words she had meant to speak to set a death-binding against him. She could only endure the hot agony, and the knowledge that she had failed—

—and then looked up in time to see three arrows strike him almost simultaneously, two in the chest, the third in the throat. Her hands clenched on the dagger hilt as he collapsed on top of her with a strangling gurgle. Agony drove her down into darkness.

Her last conscious thought was of gratitude to Lyran.

There were frogs and insects singing, which seemed odd to Martis. No one mentioned frogs or insects in any version of the afterlife that she'd ever heard. As her hearing improved, she could hear nightbirds in the distance, and close at hand, the sound of a fire and the stirring of nearby horses. That definitely did not fit in with the afterlife—unless one counted Hellfires, and this certainly didn't sound big enough to be one of those. Her eyes opened slowly, gritty and sore, and not focusing well.

Lyran sat by her side, anxiety lining his brow and exhaustion graying his face.

"Either I'm alive," Martis coughed, "or you're dead—and I don't remember you being dead."

"You live, Mage-lady—but it was a very near thing. Almost, I did not reach you in time. You are fortunate that sorcerers are not weapons-trained—no swordsman would have missed your heart as Kelven did."

"Martis. My name is Martis—you've earned the right to use it," Martis coughed again, amazed that there was so little pain—that the worst she felt was a vague ache in her lungs, a dreamy lassitude and profound weakness. "Why am I still alive? Even if he missed the heart, that blow was enough to kill. You're no Healer—" she paused, all that Lyran had told her about his "Way" running through her mind. "—are you?"

"As my hands deal death, so they must also preserve life," Lyran replied. "Yes, among my people, all who live by weapons are also trained as Healers, even as Healers must learn to use weapons, if only to defend themselves and the wounded upon the field of battle."

He rubbed eyes that looked as red and sore as her own felt. "Since I am not Healer-born, it was hard, very hard. I am nearly as weak as you as a consequence. It will be many days before I regain my former competence, my energy, or my strength. It is well you have no more enemies that I must face, for I would do so, I fear, on my hands and knees!"

Martis frowned. "You aren't talking the way you used to."

Lyran chuckled. "It is said that even when at the point of death the Mage will observe and record—and question. Yes, I use familiar speech with you, my Mage-lady. The Healing for one not born to the Gift is not like yours—I sent my soul into your body to heal it; for a time we were one. That is why I am so wearied. You are part of myself as a consequence—and I now speak to you as one of my People."

"Thank the gods. I was getting very tired of your everlasting 'this one's.' " They laughed weakly together, before Martis broke off with another fit of coughing.

"What happens to you when we get back to the Guild-hold?" Martis asked presently.

"My continued employment by the Guild was dependent on your satisfaction with my performance," Lyran replied. "Since I assume that you are satisfied—"

"I'm alive, aren't I? The mission succeeded. I'm a good bit more than merely 'satisfied' with the outcome."

"Then I believe I am to become part of the regular staff, to be assigned to whatever mage happens to need a guard. And—I think here I have found what I sought for; the place where my sword may serve peace, the place the Way has designed for me." Despite his contented words, his eyes looked wistful

Martis was feeling unwontedly sensitive to the nuances in his expression. There was something behind those words she had not expected—hope— longing? And—directed at *her*?

And—under the weariness, was there actually *desire*?

"Would that I could continue in your service, Mage—Martis. I think perhaps we deal well together."

"Hmm," Martis began tentatively, not sure she was reading him correctly; not daring to believe what she thought she saw. "As a master, I'm entitled to a permanent hireling, I just never exercised the privilege. Would you be interested?"

"As a hireling—only? Or, could I hope you would have more of me than bought-service?"

Dear gods, was he asking what she *thought* he was asking?

"Lyran, you surely can't be seriously propositioning me?" she blurted out in astonishment.

"We have been one," he sighed, touching her cheek lightly. "As you have felt a tie to me, so have

I felt drawn to you. There is that in each of us that satisfies a need in the other, I think. I—care for you. I would gladly be a friend; more than friend, if you choose."

"But I'm old enough to be your mother!"

"Ah, lady," he smiled, his eyes old in his young face, "What are years? Illusion. Do each of us not know the folly of illusion?" And he cupped one hand gently beneath her cheek to touch his lips to hers.

As her mouth opened beneath his, she was amazed at the stirring of passion—it was impossible, but it was plainly there, despite years, wounds, and weariness. Maybe—maybe there was something to this after all.

"I—" she began, then chuckled.

"Ah?" He cocked his head to one side, and waited for enlightenment.

"Well—my friends will think I'm insane, but this certainly fits your Way of Balance—my gray hairs against your youth."

"So—" The smile warmed his eyes in a way Martis found fascinating, and totally delightful, "—then we shall confound your friends, who lack your clear sight. We shall seek Balance together. Yes?"

She stretched out her hand a little to touch his, already feeling some of her years dissolving before that smile.

"Oh, yes."

Dragon's Teeth

by Mercedes Lackey

Trebenth, broad of shoulder and red of hair and beard, was Guard-serjant to the Mage Guild. Not to put too fine a point on it, he was Guard-serjant at High Ridings, *the* chief citadel of the Mage Guild, and site of the Academe Arcanum, *the* institution of Highest Magicks. As such, *he* was the warrior responsible for the safety and well-being of the Mages he served.

This was hardly the soft post that the uninformed thought it to be. Mages had many enemies—and were terribly vulnerable to physical attack. It only took one knife in the dark to kill a mage—Trebenth's concern was to circumvent that vulnerability; by overseeing their collective safety in High Ridings, or their individual safety by means of the bodyguards he picked and trained to stand watchdog over them.

And there were times when his concern for their well-being slid over into areas that had nothing to do with arms and assassinations.

This was looking—to his worried eyes, at least—like one of those times.

He was standing on the cold granite of the landing at the top of a set of spiraling tower stairs, outside a particular tower apartment in the Guild-members Hall, the highest apartment in a tower reserved for the Masterclass Mages. Sunlight poured through a skylight above him, reflecting off the pale wooden paneling of the wall he faced. There was no door at the head of this helical staircase; there *had* been one, but the occupant of the apartment had spelled it away, presumably so that her privacy *could not* be violated. But although Trebenth could not enter, he *could* hear something of what was going on beyond that fea-tureless paneled wall.

Masterclass Sorceress Martis Orleva Kiriste of High Ridings, a chief instructress of the Academe, and a woman of *at least* equal Trebenth's middle years was—giggling. Giggling like a giddy adoles-cent.

Mart hasn't been the same since she faced down Kelven, Ben gloomed, shifting his weight restlessly from his left foot to his right. *I thought at first it was just because she hadn't recovered yet from that stab-wound. Losing that much blood—gods, it would be enough to fuddle any-one's mind for a while. Then I thought it was emotional backlash from having been forced to kill somebody that was almost a substitute child for her. But then—she started acting odder in-stead of saner. First she requisitioned that out-lander as her own, and then installed him in her quarters—and is making no secret that she's installed him in her bed as well. It's like she's lost whatever sense of proportion she had.*

Behind the honey-colored paneling Trebenth heard another muffled giggle, and his spirits slipped another notch. *I thought I'd finally found her the perfect bodyguard with that outlander Lyran; one that wouldn't get in her way. He was so quiet, so—so humble. Was it all a trick to worm his way into some woman's confidence? What the hell did I really bring in? What did I let latch onto her soul?*

He shifted his weight again, sweating with indecision. Finally he couldn't bear it any longer, and tapped with one knuckle, uncharacteristically hesitant, in the area where the door *had* been.

"Go away," Martis called, the acid tone of her low voice clearly evident even through the muffling of the wood. "I am *not* on call. Go pester Uthedre."

"Mart?" Ben replied unhappily. "It's Ben. It isn't—"

There was a shimmer of golden light, and the door popped into existence under his knuckles, in the fleeting instant of time between one tap and the next. Then it swung open so unexpectedly that he was left stupidly tapping empty air.

Beyond the door was Martis' sitting room; a tiny room, mostly taken up by a huge brown couch with overstuffed cushions. Two people were curled close together there, half-disappearing into the soft pillows. One was a middle-aged, square-faced woman, graying blond hair twined into long braids that kept coming undone. Beside her was a slender young man, his shoulder-length hair nearly the color of dark amber, his obliquely slanted eyes black and unfathomable. He looked—to Trebenth's mind—fully young enough to be Martis' son. In point of fact, he was her hireling bodyguard—and her lover.

43

"Ben, you old goat!" Martis exclaimed from her seat on the couch, "Why didn't you say it was you in the first place? I'd never lock you out, no matter what, but you *know* I'm no damn good at aura-reading."

To Trebenth's relief, Martis was fully and decently clothed, as was the young outland fighter Lyran seated beside her. She lowered the hand she'd used to gesture the door back into reality and turned the final flourish into a beckoning crook of her finger. With no little reluctance Trebenth sidled into the sun-flooded outermost room of her suite. She cocked her head to one side, her gray eyes looking suspiciously mischievous and bright, her generous mouth quirked in an expectant half-smile.

"Well?" she asked. "I'm waiting to hear what you came all the way up to my tower to ask."

Trebenth flushed. "It's—about—"

"Oh, my, you sound embarrassed. Bet I can guess. Myself and my far-too-young lover, hmm?"

"Mart!" Ben exclaimed, blushing even harder. "I—didn't—"

"Don't bother, Ben," she replied, lounging back against the cushions, as Lyran watched his superior with a disconcertingly serene and thoughtful expression on his lean face. "I figured it was all over High Ridings by now. Zaila's Toenails! Why is it that when some old goat of a *man* takes a young wench to his bed everyone chuckles and considers it a credit to his virility, but when an old *woman*—"

"You are *not* old," Lyran interrupted her softly, in an almost musical tenor.

"Flatterer," she said, shaking her head at him.

"I know better. So, why is it when an *older* woman does the same, everyone figures her mind is going?"

Trebenth was rather at a loss to answer that far-too-direct question.

"Never mind, let it go. I suspect, though, that you're worried about what I've let leech onto me. Let me ask you a countering question. Is Lyran causing trouble? Acting up? Flaunting status—spending my gold like water? Boasting about his connections or—his 'conquest'?"

"Well," Ben admitted slowly. "No. He acts just like he did before; so quiet you hardly know he's there. Except—"

"Except what?"

"Some of the others have been goin' for *him*. At practice, mostly."

"And?" Beside her, Lyran shifted, and laid his right hand unobtrusively—but protectively—over the one of hers resting on the brown couch cushion between them.

"Everything stayed under control until this morning. Harverth turned the dirty side of his tongue on you 'stead of Lyran, seeing as he wasn't gettin' anywhere baiting the boy. Harverth was armed, Lyran wasn't."

Martis raised one eyebrow. "So? What happened?"

"I was gonna mix in, but they finished it before I could get involved. It didn't take long. Harverth's with the Healers. They tell me he *might* walk without limping in a year or so, but they won't promise. Hard to Heal shattered kneecaps."

Martis turned a reproachful gaze on the young, long-haired man beside her. Lyran flushed. "Pardon," he murmured. "This one was angered for

45

your sake more than this one knew. This one lost both Balance and temper."

"You lost more'n that, boy," Ben growled. "You lost me a trained—"

"—blowhard," Martis interrupted him. "You forget that you assigned that dunderhead to me once—he's damned near useless, and he's a pain in the aura to a mage like me. You know damned well you've been on the verge of kicking that idiot out on his rear a half dozen times—you've told me so yourself! Well, now you've got an excuse to pension him off—it was *my* hireling and *my* so-called honor involved; deduct the bloodprice from my account and throw the bastard out of High Ridings. There, are you satisfied?

Ben wasn't. "Mart," he said pleadingly, "it's not just that—"

"What is it? The puppies in your kennel still likely to go for Lyran?"

"No, not after this morning."

"What is it then? Afraid I'm going to become a laughingstock? Got news for you, Ben, I already *am*, and I don't give a damn. Or are you afraid *for* me, afraid that I'm making a fool of myself?"

Since that was exactly what Trebenth *had* been thinking, he flushed again, and averted *his* eyes from the pair on the sofa.

"Ben," Martis said softly, "When have you ever seen us acting as anything other than mage and hireling outside of my quarters? Haven't we at least kept the appearance of respectability?"

"I guess," he mumbled, hot with embarrassment.

"People would be talking even if there was *nothing* between us. They've talked about me ever since I got my Mastery. There were years at the beginning when everybody was *certain* I'd earned it in bed, not in the circles. And when you and I—they talked about that, too, didn't they? The only difference now is that I'm about half again older than Lyran. People just don't seem to like that, much. But my position is in no danger. When the push comes, it's my power the Guild cares about, not what damage I do to an already dubious reputation. And *I* don't care. I'm happy, maybe for the first time in years. Maybe in my life."

He looked up sharply. "Are you? Really? Are you sure?"

"I'm sure," she replied with absolute candor, as Lyran raised his chin slightly, and his eyes silently dared his superior to challenge the statement.

Trebenth sighed, and felt a tiny, irrational twinge of jealousy. After all, *he* had Margwynwy—

—but *he'd* never been able to bring that particular shine to Martis' eyes—not even at the height of their love affair.

"All right, then," he said, resigned. "As long as you don't care about the gossip—"

"Not in the slightest."

"I guess I was out of line."

"No, Ben," Martis replied fondly. "You're a friend. Friends worry about friends; I'm glad you care enough to worry. My wits haven't gone south, honestly."

"Then—I guess I'll go see about paying a certain slacker off and pitching him out."

Martis gestured the door closed behind the towering Guard-serjant, then removed the door with another gesture, and turned back to her seatmate with frustration in her eyes. "Why didn't you tell me that you were being harassed?"

Lyran shook his head; his light brown hair shimmered in the warm sun pouring through the skylight above his head. "It didn't matter. Words are only as worthy as the speaker."

"It got beyond words."

"I am better than anyone except the Guildserjant." It wasn't a boast, Martis knew, but a plain statement of fact. "What did I have to fear from harassment? It was only—" It was Lyran's turn to flush, although he continued to hold her gaze with his own eyes. "I could not bear to hear you insulted."

Something rather atavistic deep down inside her glowed with pleasure at his words. "So you leapt to my defense, hmm."

"How could I not? Martis—lady—love—" His eyes warmed to her unspoken approval.

She laughed, and leaned into the soft cushion behind her. "I suppose I'm expected to reward my defender now, hmm? Now that you've fought for my honor?"

He chuckled, and shook his head. "Silly and primitive of us, doubtless, but it does rouse up certain instinctive responses, no?"

She slid a little closer on the couch, and reached up to lace the fingers of both hands behind his neck, under his long hair. Not even the silk of his tunic was as soft as that wonderful hair. . . .

"You know good and well how I feel." The healing-magic of his people that he had used to save her life had bound their souls together; that was the reason why Lyran did *not* refer to himself in the third person when they were alone together. And it was why each tended to know now a little of what the other felt. It would have been rather futile to deny her feelings even if she'd wanted to . . . which she didn't.

"*Are* you happy, my Mage-lady?" She felt an unmistakable twinge of anxiety from him. "*Do* the words of fools hurt you? If they do—"

"They don't," she reassured him, coming nearer to him so that she could hold him closer and bury her face in that wonderful, magical hair. She wondered now how she could ever have thought it too long, and untidy, or why she had thought him effeminate. She breathed in the special scent of him; a hint of sunlight and spicy grasses. And she felt the tension of anxiety inside him turn to tension of another kind. His hands, strong yet gentle, slid around her waist and drew her closer still.

But a few hours later came a summons she could not ignore; a mage-message from the Council. And the moment the two of them passed her threshold it would have been impossible for anyone to have told that they were lovers from their demeanor. Martis was no mean actress—she was diplomat and teacher as well as sorceress, and both those professions often required the ability to play a part. And Lyran, with his incredible *mental* discipline, and a degree of training in control that matched and was in fact incorporated in his physical training, could have passed for an ice-sculpture. Only Martis could know for certain that his chill went no deeper than the surface.

He was her bodyguard; he was almost literally her possession until and unless he chose not to

serve her. And as such he went with her everywhere—even into the hallows of the Council chamber. Just as the bodyguards of the five Councillors
did.

The carved double doors of a wood so ancient as
to have turned black swung open without a hand
touching them, and she and Lyran entered the
windowless Council Chamber. It was lit entirely
by mage-lights as ancient as the doors, all still
burning with bright yellow incandescence high
up on the walls of white marble. The room was
perfectly circular and rimmed with a circle of mal-
achite; in the center was a second circle inlaid in
porphyry in the white marble of the floor. Behind
that circle was the half-circle of the Council table,
of black-laquered wood, and the five matching
thronelike chairs behind it. All five of those chairs
were occupied by mages in the purple robes of
the Mage-Guild Council.

Only one of the Councillors, the cadaverous
Masterclass Mage Ronethar Gethry, gave Lyran so
much as a glance; and from the way Ronethar's
eyes flickered from Lyran to Martis and back, the
sorceress rather guessed that it was because of
the gossip that he noticed her guard at all.

The rest ignored the swordsman, as they ignored their own hirelings, each standing impas-
sively behind his master's chair, garbed from head
to toe, as was Lyran, in Mage-Guild hireling red;
red leathers, red linen—even one, like Lyran, in
red silk.

The Councillors were worried; even Martis could
read that much behind their impassive masks.
They wasted no time on petty nonsense about her

private life. What brought them all to the Council Chamber was serious business, not accusations about whom she was dallying with.

Not that they'd dare take *her* to task over it. She was the equal of any of the mages in those five seats; she could sit there behind the Council table any time she chose. She simply had never chosen to do so. They knew it, and she knew it, and they knew she knew. She was not accountable to them, or to anything but her conscience, for her behavior. Only for her actions as a representative of the Guild.

The fact was that she didn't *want* a Council seat; as a Masterclass mage she had little enough freedom as it was. Sitting on the Council would restrict it still further. The Masterclass mage served only the Guild, the powers of the Masterclass being deemed too dangerous to be put at hire.

"Martis," rotund old Dabrel was serving as Chief this month; he was something less of an old stick than the others.

"Councillor," she responded. "How may I serve my Guild?"

"By solving a mystery," he replied. "The people of Lyosten have been acting in a most peculiar and disturbing fashion—"

"He means they've been finding excuses to put off a Guild inspection," sour-faced and acid-voiced Liavel interrupted. "First there was a fever—so they say—then a drought, then the road was blocked by a flood. It doesn't ring true; nobody else around Lyosten is having any similar troubles. We believe they're hiding something."

"Lyosten is a Free City, isn't it?" Martis asked. "Who's in charge?"

"The Citymaster—a man called Bolger Freedman."

"Not a Guildsman. A pity. That means we can't put pressure on him through his own Guild," Martis mused. "You're right, obviously; they must be covering up *something*, so what's the guess?"

"We think," Dabrel said, leaning over the table and steepling his fingertips together, "that their local mage has gone renegade in collusion with the townsfolk; that he's considering violating the Compacts against using magecraft in offensive manner against nonmages. They've been feuding off and on with Portravus for decades; we think they may be deciding to end the feud."

"And Portravus has no mage—" said mousy Herjes, looking as much frightened as worried. "Just a couple of hedge-wizards and some assorted Low Magick practitioners. And not a lot of money to spare to hire one."

Martis snorted. "*Just* what I wanted to hear. Why me?"

You're known," replied Dabrel. "They don't dare cause you any overt magical harm. You're one of the best at offensive and defensive magicks. Furthermore, you can activate the Gates to get in fairly close to the town *before* they can think up another excuse. We'll inform them that you're coming about a day before you're due to arrive."

"And there's another factor," creaked ancient Cetallas. "Your hireling. The boy is good; damned good. Best I've seen in—can't remember when. No Free City scum is going to get past *him* to take you out. He's a healer of sorts, so Ben tells us. That's no bad thing to have about, a healer you can trust just in case some physical accident happens. And you must admit he's got a pretty powerful incentive to keep you alive." The old man wheezed a little, and quirked an amused eyebrow at the two of them. Martis couldn't help notice the twinkle of laughter in his eyes. She bit her lip to keep from smiling. So the old bird still had some juice in him—and wasn't going to grudge her *her* own pleasures!

"You have a point," she admitted. "And yes, Lyran does have something more at stake with me than just his contract." She was rather surprised to see the rest of the Councillors nod soberly.

Well. Well, well! They may not like it—they may think I'm some kind of fool, or worse—but they've got to admit that what Lyran and I have can be pretty useful to the Guild. "How soon do you want us to leave?"

"Are you completely recovered from—"

"Dealing with Kelven? Physically, yes. Mentally, emotionally—to be honest, only time will tell. Betrayal; gods, that's not any easy thing to deal with. . . ."

"Admitted—and we're setting you up to deal with another traitor." Dabrel had the grace to look guilty.

"At least this one isn't one of my former favorite pupils," she replied, grimacing crookedly, "I don't even think I know him."

"You don't," Herjes said, "I trained him. He also is not anywhere near Kelven's potential, and he *isn't* dabbling in blood-magic. Speaking of which— have you recovered arcanely as well as physically?"

"I'm at full power. I can go any time."

"In the morning, then?"

"In the morning." She inclined her head slightly; felt the faintest whisper of magic brush her by.

Show-offs, she thought, as she heard the doors behind her open. *Two can play that game.*

"We will be on our way at dawn, Councillors," she said, carefully setting up the *rolibera* spell in her mind, and wrapping it carefully about both herself *and* Lyran. There weren't too many mages even at Masterclass level that could translate two people at once. She braced herself, formed the energy into a tightly coiled spring with her mind, then spoke one word as she inclined her head again—

There was a flash of light behind her eyes, and a fluttery feeling in her stomach as if she had suddenly dropped the height of a man.

And she and Lyran stood side-by-side within the circle carved into the floor of her private workroom.

She turned to see the mask of indifference drop from him and his thin, narrow face come alive with mingled humor and chiding.

"Can you not stop challenging them, beloved?"

She set her mouth stubbornly. He shook his head. "Alas," he chuckled, "I fear if you did, I would no longer know you. Challenge and avoidance—" He held out his arms, and she flowed into them. "Truly, beloved," he murmured into her ear, as she pressed her cheek into the silk of his tunic shoulder, "We Balance each other."

They would not be riding Jesalis and Tosspot, those beasts of foul temper and fiercely protective instincts. This was a mission which would depend as much on the impression they would give as on their capabilities, and Tosspot and Jesalis would be unlikely to impress anyone. Instead, when they descended the tower stairs in the pale, pearly light of dawn, Martis found the grooms in the stone-paved courtyard holding the reins of two showy palfreys, a gray and a bay. Tethered behind the bay on a lead rope was a glossy mule loaded with packs. The harness of the gray was dyed a rich purple, and that of the bay was scarlet. Lyran approached the horses with care, for the eyes of the bay rolled with alarm at the sight of the stranger. He ran his hands over their legs once he could get near them, and walked slowly back to Martis' side with his arms folded, shaking his head a little.

"Hmm?" she asked.

"Worthless," he replied. "I hope we will not be needing to entrust our lives to them. No strength, no stamina—and worst of all, no sense."

"They're just for show," Martis frowned, feeling a little dubious herself. "We aren't supposed to have to do any hard riding, or long, except for the gallop to take us through the Gates. A day's ride to the first Gate, half a day to the second. In and out of both Gates, then a ride of less than half a day to the city. . . ."

"If all goes well. And what if all does not go well?"

"I—" Martis fell silent. "Well, that's why you're along."

Lyran looked back over his shoulder at the horses, and grimaced. "This one will do the best one can, Mage-lady," he said formally. "Will the Mage-lady mount?"

Martis had been doing more with Lyran's aid than her colleagues suspected. A few moons ago she would not have been able to mount unaided—

55

now she swung into her saddle with at least some of the grace of her lover. The exercises he had been insisting she practice had improved her strength, her wind, her flexibility—she was nearly as physically fit as she'd been twenty-odd years ago, when she'd first come to the Academe.

Lyran mounted at nearly the same moment, and his bay tried to shy sideways. It jerked the reins out of the groom's hands, and danced backward, then reared. Lyran's mouth compressed, but that was the only sign that he was disturbed that Martis could see. The scarlet silk of his breeches rippled as he clamped his legs around the bay gelding's barrel, and the reins seemed to tighten of themselves as he forced the gelding back down to the ground, and fought him to a standstill. As the horse stood, sweating, sides heaving, Lyran looked up at her.

"This one will do what this one can, Mage-lady," he repeated soberly.

The gray palfrey Martis rode was of a more placid disposition, for which she was profoundly grateful. She signed to the groom to release his hold and turned its head to face the open wooden gate set into the stone walls of the court. At Lyran's nod she nudged it with her heels and sent it ambling out beneath the portcullis.

They rode in single file through the city, Lyran trailing the mule at a respectful distance from "his employer." Four times the bay started and shied at inconsequential commonplaces; each time Lyran had to fight the beast back onto all four hooves and into sweating good behavior. The last time seemed to convince it that there was no unseating its rider, for it did not make another attempt.

Once outside the city walls, they reversed their positions, with Lyran and the mule going first. Ordinarily Martis would now be spending her time in half-trance, gathering power from the living things around her. But her mount was *not* her faithful Tosspot, who could be relied upon to keep a falling-down drunk in the saddle—and Lyran's beast was all too likely to shy or dance again, and perhaps send her gelding off as well.

So instead of gathering always-useful energy, she fumed and fretted, and was too annoyed even to watch the passing landscape.

They reached the Gate at sunset. The ring of standing stones in the center of the meadow stood out black against the flaming glow of the declining sun. The wide, weed-grown fields around them were otherwise empty; not even sheep cared to graze this near a Gate. The evening wind carried a foretaste of autumnal chill as it sighed through the grasses around them. Martis squinted against the bloody light and considered their options.

Lyran had finally decided to exhaust his misbehaving mount by trotting it in circles around her as they traveled down the road until it was too tired to fuss. Now it was docile, but plainly only because it was weary. It still rolled its eyes whenever a leaf stirred.

The sorceress urged her gelding up beside him. "Can you get one last run out of him?" Martis asked anxiously.

"Probably," Lyran replied. "Why?"

"I'd like to take this Gate now, if we can, while that misbegotten horse of yours is too tired to bolt."

He looked at her in that silent, blank-faced way he had when he was thinking. "What if he did bolt?"

"The gods only know where you'd end up," she told him frankly. "If he got out of my influence—I can't predict what point beyond the Gate you'd come out at, or even what direction it would be in."

"And if I can't get him to a gallop?"

"Almost the same—if you didn't keep within my aura you'd come out somewhere between here and where I'd land."

He reached out and touched her face with the tips of his fingers. "You seem tired, beloved."

"I *am* tired," she admitted, confessing to him what she would admit to no other living person. "But I'm not too tired to Gate-spell, and I think it's safer to do it now than it will be later."

"Then I will force this bundle of contrariness disguised as a horse into keeping up with you."

"Hold butter-brains here, would you?" She passed him the reins of her mount, not trusting it to stand firm on its own. She drew entirely into herself, centering all her concentration on the hoarded power within herself, drawing it gradually to the surface with unspoken words and careful mental probes. Her eyes were closed, but she could feel the energy stirring, flowing, coming up from—elsewhere—and beginning to trickle along the nerves of her spine. At first it was barely a tingle, but the power built up quickly until she was vibrating to its silent song.

At that point she opened the channels to her hands, raising her arms out in front of her and holding her hands out with the open palms facing the ring of standing stones.

The power surged along her arms and leapt for the ring of the Gate with an eagerness that was almost an emotion. She sang the words of the Gate-spell now, sang it in a barely audible whisper. Her eyes were half open, but she really wasn't paying a great deal of attention to anything but the flow of power from her to the Gate.

The ring of stones began to glow, glowing as if they were stealing the last of the sun's fire and allowing it to run upon their surfaces. The color of the fire began to lighten, turning from deep red to scarlet to a fiery orange. Then the auras surrounding each Gate-stone extended; reaching for, then touching, the auras beside it, until the circle became one pulsating ring of golden-orange light.

Martis felt the proper moment approaching, and signed to Lyran to hand her back her reins. She waited, weighing, judging—then suddenly spurred her mount into one of the gaps between the stones, with Lyran's gelding practically on top of her horse's tail.

They emerged into a forest clearing beneath a moon already high, exactly five leagues from the next Gate.

"Gods, I wish I had Tosspot under me," Martis muttered, facing the second Gate under a bright noontide sun. This one stood in the heart of the forest, and the stones were dwarfed by the stand of enormous pine trees that towered all about them. The sorceress was feeling depleted, and she had not been able to recuperate the energy she'd spent on the last spell.

"We could wait," Lyran suggested. "We could rest here, and continue on in the morning."

Martis shook her head with regret. "I only wish we could. But it isn't healthy to camp near a Gate—look at the way the magic's twisted those bushes over there, the ones growing up against the stones! And besides, we need to come as close to surprising our hosts as we can."

She coughed; there was a tickle in the back of her throat that threatened to turn into a cold. Lyran noted that cough, too, and tightened his mouth in unvoiced disapproval, but made no further objections. Martis handed him her reins, and began the second spell—

But they emerged, not into a sunlit clearing as she'd expected, but into the teeth of the worst storm she'd ever seen.

Rain, cold as the rains of winter, lashed at them, soaking them to the skin in moments. It would have been too dark to see, except that lightning struck so often that the road was clearly lit most of the time. Lyran spurred his horse up beside the sorceress as she gasped for breath beneath the onslaught of the icy water. He'd pulled his cloak loose from the lashings that held it to his saddle and was throwing it over her shoulders before she even had recovered the wit to _think_ about the fact that she needed it. The cloak was sodden in seconds, but it was wool—warm enough, even though wet. She stopped shivering a little, but the shock of chill coming on top of the strain of the spells had unbalanced her a little. She fumbled after her reins, but her mind wouldn't quite work; she couldn't seem to think where they should be going.

Lyran put his hand under her chin, and turned her face toward his. She blinked at him, at his searching expression as revealed by the flickers of lightning. Some rational little bit of her that hadn't been stunned hoped idly that he remembered what she'd told him once, about how mages sometimes went into spell-shock when they were low on energy and hit with unexpected physical conditions. This happened most frequently when they were ungrounded and uncentered—and the Gate-spell demanded that she be both when taking them in transit.

Evidently he did, for he took the reins out of her unresisting fingers and nudged his gelding into a nervy, shuddering walk, leaving her to cling to the saddle as best she could while he led her mount.

It was impossible to hear or be heard over the nearly continuous roar of the thunder, so she didn't even try to speak to him. She just closed her eyes and concentrated on getting herself centered and grounded again.

So it was that she never noticed when the road approached the brink of a river—once peaceful, now swollen and angry with flood water. She knew that there *was* such a road, and such a river— she knew that they were to cross it before reaching Lyosten. She knew that there was a narrow, aged bridge that was still nonetheless sound, but she was too deeply sunk within herself to see it, as Lyran urged the horses onto its span.

But she *felt* the lightning strike, so close it scorched the wood of the bridge not ten paces in front of them.

And as her eyes snapped open, she saw Lyran's

horse rearing above her in complete panic—a darkly writhing shape that reared and thrashed—and toppled over onto *hers*. She had no time to react; she felt herself go numb and open-mouthed in fear, and then pain as all of them, horses, humans, and mule, crashed through the railing of the bridge to plunge into the churning water below. She flailed wildly with unfocused energy trying to form up something to catch them—and lost spell and all in the shock of hitting the raging water.

Martis pulled herself up onto the muddy bank, scraping herself across the rocks and tree-roots protruding from it, and dragging Lyran with her by the shoulder-fabric of his tunic. She collapsed, half-in, half-out of the water, too spent to go any farther. The swordsman pulled himself, coughing, up onto the bank beside her. A child of open plains, *he* couldn't swim.

Fortunately for both of them, Martis could. And equally fortunately, he'd had the wit to go limp when he felt her grabbing his tunic.

The storm—now that the damage was done—was slackening.

"Are you all right?" she panted, turning her head and raising herself on her arms enough to be able to see him, while her teeth chattered like temple rattles.

Lyran had dragged himself up into a sitting position, and was clutching a sapling as if it was a lover. His eyes were bruised and swollen, one of them almost shut, and there was a nasty welt along the side of his face. He coughed, swallowed, nodded. "I think—yes."

"Good." She fell back onto the bank, cheek pressed into the mud, trying to keep from coughing herself. If she did—it felt as if she might well cough her aching lungs out. She fought the cough with closed eyes, the rain plastering hair and clothing flat to her skin.

This is witched weather; the power is everywhere, wild, undisciplined. How could that Lyosten mage have let himself get so out of control?

But that was just a passing thought, unimportant. The important thing was the cold, the aching weariness. She was so cold now that she had gone beyond feeling it—

"Martis—"

She was drifting, drifting away, being carried off somewhere where there was sun and warmth. In fact, she was actually beginning to feel warm, not cold. She felt Lyran shake her shoulder, and didn't care. All she wanted to do was sleep. She'd never realized how soft mud could be.

"Martis!" It was the sharp-edged fear in his voice as much as the stinging slap he gave her that woke her. She got her eyes open with difficulty.

"What?" she asked stupidly, unable to think.

"Beloved, *thena*, you are afire with fever," he said, pulling her into his arms and chafing her limbs to get the blood flowing. "I cannot heal disease, only wounds. Fight this—you must fight this, or you will surely die!"

"Ah—" she groaned, and tried to pummel the fog that clouded her mind away. But it was a battle doomed to be lost; she felt the fog take her, and drifted away again.

* * *

Lyran half-carried, half-dragged the mage up the last few feet of the road to the gates of Lyosten. The horses were gone, and the mule, and with them everything except what they had carried on their persons that had not been ripped away by the flood-waters. His two swords were gone; he had only his knife, his clothing, and the money belt beneath his tunic. Martis had only her robes; no implements of magic or healing, no cloak to keep her warm—

At least she had not succumbed to shock or the cold-death; she was intermittently conscious, if not coherent. But she was ill—very ill, and like to become worse.

The last few furlongs of road had been a waking nightmare; the rain stopped as if it had been shut off, but the breeze that had sprung up had chilled them even as it had dried their clothing. Once past the thin screen of trees lining the river, there had been nothing to buffer it. It hadn't helped that Lyran could see the bulk of Lyosten looming in the distance, dark gray against a lighter gray sky. He'd forced himself and Martis into motion, but more often than not he was supporting her; sheer exhaustion made them stagger along the muddy road like a pair of drunks, getting mired to the knees in the process. It was nearly sunset when they reached the gates of the city.

He left Martis leaning against the wood of the wall and went to pound on the closed gates themselves, while she slid slowly down to crouch in a miserable huddle, fruitlessly seeking shelter from the wind.

A man-sized door opened in the greater gate, and a surly, bearded fighter blocked it.

"What's the ruckus?" he growled.

Lyran drew himself up and tried not to shiver. "This one is guard to Martis, Master Sorceress and envoy of the Mages' Guild," he replied, his voice hoarse, his throat rasping. "There has been an accident . . ."

"Sure, tell me another one," the guard jeered, looking from Lyran to the bedraggled huddle that was Martis, and back again. He started to close the portal. "You think I've never heard *that* one before? Go around to th' Beggars' Gate."

"Wait!" Lyran blocked the door with his foot, but before he could get another word out, the guard unexpectedly lashed out with the butt of his pike, catching him with a painful blow to the stomach. It knocked the wind out of him and caused him to land on his rump in the mud of the road. The door in the gate slammed shut.

Lyran lowered Martis down onto the pallet, and knelt beside her. He covered her with every scrap of ragged blanket or quilt that he could find. She was half out of her mind with fever now, and coughing almost constantly. The cheap lamp of rock-oil gave off almost as much smoke as light, which probably didn't help the coughing any.

"Martis?" he whispered, hoping against hope for a sane response.

This time he finally got one. Her eyes opened, and there was sense in them. "Lyr—" she went into a coughing fit. He helped her to sit up, and held a mug of water to her mouth. She drank, her hand pressed against his, and the hand was so hot it frightened him.

"*Thena*," he said urgently, "you are ill, very ill. I

cannot heal sickness, only hurts. Tell me what I must do."

"Take me—to the Citymaster—"

He shook his head. "I tried; they will not let me near. I cannot prove that I am what I say—"

"Gods. And I can't—magic—to prove it."

"You haven't even been answering me." He put the cup on the floor and wedged himself in behind her, supporting her. She closed her eyes as if even the dim light of the lamp hurt them. Her skin was hot and dry, and tight-feeling, as he stroked her forehead.

"The storm—witched."

"You said as much in raving, so I guessed it better to avoid looking for the city wizard. Tell me what I must do!"

"Is there—money—"

"A little. A very little."

"Get—trevaine-root. Make tea."

He started. "And poison you? Gods and demons!"

"Not poison," She coughed again. "It'll put me—where I can trance. Heal myself. Only way."

"But—"

"Only way I know," she repeated, and closed her eyes. Within moments the slackness of her muscles told him she'd drifted off into delirium again.

He lowered her back down to the pallet, and levered himself to his feet. The bed and the lamp were all the furnishings this hole of a room had; Martis had bigger closets back at High Ridings.

And he'd been lucky to find the room in the first place. The old woman who rented it to him had been the first person he'd accosted that had "felt" honest.

He blew out the lamp and made his own way down

to the street. Getting directions from his hostess, he headed for the marketplace. The ragged and threadbare folk who jostled him roused his anxiety to a fever-pitch. He sensed that many of them would willingly knife him from behind for little or no reason. He withdrew into himself, shivering mentally, and put on an icy shell of outward calm.

The streets were crowded; Lyran moved carefully within the flow of traffic, being cautious to draw no attention to himself. He was wearing a threadbare tunic and breeches nearly identical to a dozen others around him; his own mage-hireling silk was currently adorning Martis' limbs beneath her mage-robes. The silk was one more layer of covering against the chill—and he didn't like the notion of appearing in even stained mage-hireling red in public; not around here. He closed his mind to the babble and his nose to the stench of unwashed bodies, uncleaned privies, and garbage that thickened the air about him. But these people worried him; he had only his knife for defense. What if some of this street-scum should learn about Martis, and decide she was worth killing and robbing? If he had his swords, or even just a single sword of the right reach and weight, he could hold off an army—but he didn't, nor could he afford one. The only blades he'd seen within his scanty resources were not much better than cheap metal clubs.

Finally he reached the marketplace. Trevaine-root was easy enough to find, being a common rat-poison. He chose a stall whose owner "felt" reasonably honest and whose wares looked properly preserved, and began haggling.

A few moments later he slid his hand inside his tunic to extract the single coin he required from the heartbreakingly light money-belt, separating it from the others by feel. The herbalist handed over the scrap of root bound up in a bit of old paper without a second glance; Lyran hadn't bought enough to arouse suspicion. But then, it didn't take much to make a single cup of strong tea.

Lyran turned, and narrowly avoided colliding with a scarred man, a man who walked with the air of a tiger, and whose eyes were more than a little mad. Lyran ducked his head, and willed himself invisible with all his strength. If only he had a *sword!* The need was beginning to be more than an itch—it was becoming an ache.

Lyran was heading out of the market and back to the boarding-house when he felt an unmistakable mental "pull," not unlike the calling he had felt when he first was moved to take up the Way of the sword, the pull he had felt when he had chosen his Teacher. It did not "feel" wrong, or unBalanced. Rather, it was as if Something was sensing the need in him for a means to protect Martis, and was answering that need.

Hardly thinking, he followed that pull, trusting to it as he had trusted to the pull that led him to the doorstep of the woman destined to be his Teacher, and as he had followed the pull that had led him ultimately to the Mage Guild at High Ridings and to Martis. This time it led him down the twisting, crooked path of a strangely silent street, a street hemmed by tall buildings so that it scarcely saw the sun; a narrow street that was wide enough only for two people to pass abreast.

And at the end of it—for it proved to be a dead-end street, which accounted in part for the silence —was an odd little junk shop.

There were the expected bins of rags, cracked pottery pieces, the scavenged flotsam of a thousand lives. Nothing ever went to waste in this quarter. Rags could be patched together into clothing or quilts like those now covering Martis; bits of crockery were destined to be fitted and cemented into a crazy-paving that would pass as a tiled floor. Old papers went to wrap parcels, or to eke out a thinning shoe-sole. No, nothing was ever thrown away here; but there was more to this shop than junk, Lyran could sense it. People could find what they *needed* here.

"You require something, lad," said a soft voice at his elbow.

Lyran jumped—he hadn't sensed *any* presence at his side—yet there was a strange little man, scarcely half Lyran's height; a dwarf, with short legs, and blunt, clever hands, and bright, birdlike eyes. And a kindness like that of the widow who had rented them her extra room, then brought every bit of covering she had to spare to keep Martis warm.

"A sword," Lyran said hesitantly. "This one needs a sword."

"I should think you do," replied the little man, after a long moment of sizing Lyran up. "A swordsman generally does need a sword. And it can't be an ill-balanced bludgeon, either—that would be worse than nothing, eh, lad?"

Lyran nodded, slowly. "But this one—has but little—"

The man barked rather than laughed, but his

good humor sounded far more genuine than anything coming from the main street and marketplace. "Lad, if you had money, you wouldn't be *here*, now, would you? Let me see what I can do for you."

He waddled into the shop door, past the bins of rags and whatnot; Lyran's eyes followed him into the darkness of the doorway, but couldn't penetrate the gloom. In a moment, the shopkeeper was back, a long, slim shape wrapped in oily rags in both his hands. He handed the burden to Lyran with a kind of courtly flourish.

"Here you be, lad," he said, "I think that may have been what was calling you."

The rags fell away, and the little man caught them before they hit the paving stones—

At first Lyran was conscious only of disappointment. The hilt of this weapon had once been ornamented, wrapped in gold wire, perhaps—but there were empty sockets where the gems had been, and all traces of gold had been stripped away.

"Left in pawn to me, but the owner never came back, poor man," the shopkeeper said, shaking his head. "A good man fallen on hard times— unsheathe it, lad."

The blade was awkward in his hand for a moment, the hilt hard to hold with the rough metal bare in his palm—but as he pulled it from its sheath, it seemed to come almost alive; he suddenly found the balancing of it, and as the point cleared the sheath it had turned from a piece of dead metal to an extension of his arm.

He had feared that it was another of the useless dress-swords, the ones he had seen too many

70

times, worthless mild steel done up in long-gone jewels and plating. This sword—this blade had belonged to a fighter, had been made for a swordsman. The balance, the temper were almost too good to be true. It more than equaled his lost twin blades, it surpassed them. With this one blade in hand he could easily have bested a twin-Lyran armed with his old sword-pair; that was the extent of the "edge" this blade could give him.

"How—how much?" he asked, mouth dry.

"First you must answer me true," the little man said softly. "You be the lad with the sick lady, no? The one that claimed the lady to be from the Mage Guild?"

Lyran whirled, stance proclaiming that he was on his guard. The dwarf simply held out empty hands. "No harm to you, lad. No harm meant. Tell me true, and the blade's yours for three copper bits. Tell me not, or tell me lie—I won't sell it. Flat."

"What if this one is not that person?" Lyran hedged.

"So long as the answer be true, the bargain be true."

Lyran swallowed hard, and followed the promptings of his inner guides. "This one—is," he admitted with reluctance. "This one and the lady are what this one claims—but none will heed."

The dwarf held out his hand, "Three copper bits," he said mildly. "And some advice for free."

Lyran fumbled out the coins, hardly able to believe his luck. The worst pieces of pot-metal pounded into the shape of a sword were selling for a silver—yet this strange little man had sold him a blade worth a hundred times that for the price of a round of cheese! "This one never rejects advice."

"But you may or may not heed it, eh?" The man smiled, showing a fine set of startlingly white teeth. "Right enough; you get your lady to tell you the story of the dragon's teeth. Then tell her that Bolger Freedman has sown them, but can't harvest them."

Lyran nodded, though without understanding.

"There's some of us that never agreed with him. There's some of us would pay dearly to get shut of what we've managed to get into. Tell your lady that—and watch your backs. I'm not the only one who's guessed."

Lyran learned the truth of the little man's words long before he reached the widow's boarding-house.

The gang of street-toughs lying in ambush for him were probably considered canny, crafty and subtle by the standards of the area. But Lyran knew that they were there as he entered the side-street; and he knew *where* they were moments before they attacked him.

The new sword was in his hands and moving as the first of them struck at him from behind. It sliced across the thug's midsection as easily as if Lyran had been cutting bread, not flesh, and with just about as much resistance. While the bully was still falling, he took out the one dropping on him from the wall beside him with a graceful continuation of that cut, and kicked a third rushing him from out of an alley, delivering a blow to his knee that shattered the kneecap, and then forced the knee to bend in the direction opposite to that which nature had intended.

He couldn't get the blade around in time to deal with the fourth, so he ducked under the blow and brought the pommel up into the man's nose, shattering the bone and driving the splinters into the brain.

And while the fifth man stared in openmouthed stupefaction, Lyran separated his body from his head.

Before anyone could poke a curious nose into the street to see what all the noise was about, Lyran vaulted to the top of the wall to his left, and from there to the roof of the building it surrounded. He scampered quickly over the roof and down again on the other side, taking the time to clean and sheathe the sword and put it away before dropping down into the next street.

After all, he hadn't spent his childhood as a thief without learning something about finding unconventional escape routes.

About the time he had taken a half dozen paces, alarm was raised in the next street. Rather than running away, Lyran joined the crowd that gathered about the five bodies, craning his neck like any of the people around him, wandering off when he "couldn't get a look."

A childhood of thieving had taught him the truth of what his people often said: "If you would be taken for a crow, join the flock and caw."

Lyran took the cracked mug of hot water from his hostess, then shooed her gently out. He didn't want her to see—and perhaps recognize—what he was going to drop into it. She probably wouldn't understand. For that matter, *he* didn't understand; he just trusted Martis.

His lover tossed her head on the bundle of rags that passed for a pillow and muttered, her face sweat-streaked, her hair lank and sodden. He soothed her as best he could, feeling oddly helpless.

When the water was lukewarm and nearly black, he went into a half trance and soul-called her until she woke. Again—to his relief—when he finally brought her to consciousness, there was a foggy sense in her gray eyes.

"I have the tea, *thena*," he said, helping her into a sitting position. She nodded, stifling a coughing fit, and made a weak motion with her hand. Interpreting it correctly, he held the mug to her lips. She clutched at it with both hands, but her hands shook so that he did not release the mug, only let her guide it.

He lowered her again to the pallet when she had finished the foul stuff, sitting beside her and holding her hands in his.

"How long will this take?"

She shook her head. "A bit of time before the drug takes; after that, I don't know." She coughed, doubling over; he supported her.

"Have you ever known any story about 'dragon's teeth,' my lady?" he asked, reluctantly. "I—was advised to tell you that Bolger has sown the dragon's teeth, but cannot harvest them."

She shook her head slightly, a puzzled frown creasing her forehead—then her eyes widened. "Harvest! Gods! I—"

The drug chose that moment to take her; between one word and the next her eyes glazed, then closed. Lyran swore, in three languages, fluently and creatively. It was some time before he ran out of invective.

I know 'bout dragon's teeth," said a high, young voice from the half-open door behind him. Lyran jumped in startlement for the second time that day. Truly, anxiety for Martis was dulling his edge!

He turned slowly, to see the widow's youngest son peeking around the doorframe.

"And would you tell this one of dragon's teeth?" he asked the dirty-faced urchin as politely as he could manage.

Encouraged, the youngster pushed the door open a little more. "You ain't never seen a dragon?" he asked.

Lyran shook his head, and crooked his finger. The boy sidled into the room, clasping his hands behind his back. To the widow's credit, only the child's face was dirty—the cut-down tunic he wore was threadbare, but reasonably clean. "There are no dragons in this one's homeland."

"Be there mages?" the boy asked, and at Lyran's negative headshake, the child nodded. "That be why. Dragons ain't natural beasts, they be mage-made. Don't breed, neither. You want 'nother dragon, you take tooth from a live dragon an' plant it. Only thing is, baby dragons come up hungry an' mean. Takes a tamed dragon to harvest 'em, else they go out killin' and feedin' an' get the taste fer fear. Then their brains go bad, an' they gotta be killed theyselves."

"This one thanks you," Lyran replied formally. The child grinned, and vanished.

Well, now he knew about dragon's teeth. The only problem was that the information made no *sense*—at least not to him! It had evidently meant something to Martis, though. She must have some bit of information that *he* didn't have.

He stroked the mage's damp forehead and sighed. At least the stuff hadn't killed her outright—he'd been half afraid that it would. And she *did* seem to be going into a proper trance; her breathing had become more regular, her pulse had slowed—

Suddenly it was far too quiet in the street outside.

Lyran was on his feet with his new sword in his hand at nearly the same moment that he noted the absence of sound. He slipped out the door, closing it carefully behind him once he knew that the musty hallway was "safe." The stairs that led downward were at the end of that hall—but he had no intention of taking them.

Instead he glided soundlessly to the window at the other end of the hall; the one that overlooked the scrap of back yard. The shutters were open, and a careful glance around showed that the yard itself was empty. He sheathed the sword and adjusted the makeshift baldric so that it hung at his back, then climbed out onto the ledge, balancing there while he assessed his best path.

There was a cornice with a crossbeam just within reach; he got a good grip on it, and pulled himself up, chinning himself on the wood of the beam—his arms screamed at him, but he dared not make a sound. Bracing himself, he let go with his right hand and swung himself up until he caught the edge of the roof. Holding onto it with a deathgrip, he let go of the cornice entirely, got his other hand on the roof-edge, and half-pulled, half-scrambled up onto the roof itself. He lay there for one long moment, biting his lip to keep from moaning, and willing his arms back into their sockets.

When he thought he could move again, he slid over the roof across the splintery, sunwarmed shingles to the street-side, and peered over the edge.

Below him, as he had suspected, were a half-dozen armed men, all facing the door. Except for them, the street below was deserted.

There was one waiting at the blind side of the door. Lyran pulled his knife from the sheath in his boot and dropped on him.

The *crack* as the man's skull hit the pavement —he hadn't been wearing a helm—told Lyran that he wouldn't have to worry about slitting the fighter's throat.

Lyran tumbled and rolled as he landed, throwing his knife as he came up at the man he judged to be the leader. His aim was off—instead of hitting the throat it glanced off the fighter's chest-armor. But the move distracted all of them enough to give Lyran the chance to get his sword out and into his hands.

There was something wrong with these men; he knew that as soon as he faced them. They moved oddly; their eyes were not quite focused. And even in the heat of the day, when they must have been standing out in the sun for a good long time setting up their ambush, with one exception they weren't sweating.

Then Lyran noticed that, except for the man he'd thrown the dagger at—the man who *was* sweating—they weren't casting any shadows. Which meant that they were illusions. They could only harm him if he believed in them.

So he ignored them, and concentrated his attention on the leader. He went into a purely defensive stance and waited for the man to act.

The fighter, a rugged, stocky man with a wary look to his eyes, sized him up carefully—and looked as if he wasn't happy with what he saw. Neither of them moved for a long, silent moment. Finally Lyran cleared his throat, and spoke.

"This one has no quarrel with any here, nor does this one's lady. You have done your best; this one has sprung the trap. There is no dishonor in retreat. Hireling to hireling, there is no contract violation."

The man straightened, looked relieved. "You—"

"*No!*"

The voice was high, cracking a little, and came from Lyran's left, a little distance up the street. It was a young voice; a breath later the owner emerged from the shadow of a doorway, and the speaker matched the voice. It was a white-blond boy, barely adolescent, dressed in gaudy silks; from behind him stepped two more children, then another pair. All of them were under the age of fifteen, all were dressed in rainbow hues—and all of them had wild, wide eyes that looked more than a little mad.

The man facing Lyran swallowed hard; *now* he was sweating even harder. Lyran looked at him curiously. It almost seemed as if he was *afraid* of these children! Lyran decided to act.

He stepped out into the street and placed himself between the man and the group of youngsters. "There has been no contract violation," he said levelly, meeting their crazed eyes, blue and green and brown, with his own. "The man has fulfilled what was asked." Behind him, he heard the fighter take to his heels once the attention of the children had switched from himself to Lyran. Lyran sighed with relief; that was one death, at least, that he would not have to Balance. "This one has no quarrel with you," he continued, "Why seek you this one?"

The children stared at him, a kind of insane effrontery in their faces, as if they could not believe that he would defy them. Lyran stood easily, blade held loosely in both hands, waiting for their response.

The blond, nearest and tallest, raised his hands; a dagger of light darted from his outstretched palms and headed straight for Lyran's throat—

But this was something a Mage Guild fighter was trained to defend against; fire daggers could not survive the touch of cold steel—

Lyran's blade licked out, and intercepted the dagger before it reached its target. It vanished when the steel touched it.

The child snarled, his mouth twisted into a grimace of rage ill-suited to the young face. Another dagger flew from his hands, and another; his companions sent darts of light of their own. Within moments Lyran was moving as he'd never moved in his life, dancing along the street, his swordblade blurring as he deflected dagger after dagger.

And still the fire-daggers kept coming, faster and faster—yet—

The air was growing chill, the sunlight thinning, and the faces of the children losing what little color they had possessed. Lyran realized then that they were draining themselves and everything about them for the energy to create the daggers. Even as the realization occurred to him, one of them made a choking sound and collapsed to the pavement, to lie there white and still.

If he could just hold out long enough, he *might* be able to outlast them!

But the eldest of the group snarled when his confederate collapsed, and redoubled his efforts. Lyran found himself being pressed back, the light-daggers coming closer and closer before he was able to intercept them, his arms becoming leaden and weary—

He knew then that he would fail before they did.

And he saw, as he deflected a blade heading for his heart, another heading for his throat—and he knew he would not be able to intercept this one.

He had an instant to wonder if it would hurt very much.

Then there was a blinding flash of light.

He wasn't dead—only half-blind for a long and heart-stopping moment. And when his eyes cleared—

Martis stood in the doorway of the house that had sheltered them, bracing herself against the frame, her left palm facing him, her right, the children. Both he and the youngsters were surrounded by a haze of light; his was silver, theirs was golden.

Martis gestured, and the haze around him vanished. He dropped to the pavement, so weak with weariness that his legs could no longer hold him. She staggered over to his side, weaving a little.

"Are you going to be all right?" she asked. He nodded, panting. Her hair was out of its braids, and stringy with sweat, her robes limp with it. She knelt beside him for a moment; placed both her hands on his shoulders and looked long and deeply into his eyes. "Gods, love—that was close. Too close. Did they hurt you?"

He shook his head, and she stared at him as he'd sometimes seen her examine something for magic taint. Evidently satisfied by what she saw, she kissed him briefly and levered herself back up onto her feet.

His eyes blurred for a moment; when they refocused, he saw that the haze around the remaining four children had vanished, and that they had collapsed in a heap, crying, eyes no longer crazed. Martis stood, shoulders sagging just a little, a few paces away from them.

She cleared her throat. The eldest looked up, face full of fear—

But she held out her arms to them. "It wasn't your fault," she said, in a voice so soft only the children and Lyran could have heard the words, and so full of compassion Lyran scarcely recognized it. "I know it wasn't your fault—and I'll help you, if you let me."

The children froze—then stumbled to their feet and surrounded her, clinging to her sweat-sodden robes, and crying as if their hearts had been broken, then miraculously remended.

"—so Bolger decided that he had had enough of the Mage Guild dictating what mages could and could not do. He waited until the Lyosten wizard had tagged the year's crop of mage-Talented younglings, then had the old man poisoned."

The speaker was the dwarf—who Lyran now knew was one of the local earth-witches, a cheerful man called Kasten Ythres. They were enjoying the hospitality of his home while the Mage Guild dealt with the former Citymaster and the clutch of half-trained children he'd suborned.

Martis was lying back against Lyran's chest, wearily at ease within the protective circle of his arms. They were both sitting on the floor, in one corner by the fireplace in the earth-witch's common room; there were no furnishings here, just piles of flat pillows. Martis had found it odd, but it had reminded Lyran strongly of home.

It was an oddly charming house, like its owner; brown and warm and sunny; utterly unpretentious. Kasten had insisted that they relax and put off their mage-hireling act. "It's my damned house," he'd said, "and you're my guests. To the nether hells with so-called propriety!"

"How on earth did he think he was going to get them trained?" Martis asked.

Kasten snorted. "He thought he could do it out of books—and if that didn't work, he'd get one of us half-mages to do it for him. Fool."

"He sowed the dragon's teeth," Martis replied acidly. "He shouldn't have been surprised to get dragons."

"Lady—dragon's teeth?" Lyran said plaintively, still at a loss to understand.

Martis chuckled, and settled a little more comfortably against Lyran's shoulder. "I was puzzled for a moment, too, until I remembered that the storm that met us had been witched—and that the power that created it was out of control. Magic power has some odd effects on the mind, love—if you *aren't* being watched over and guided properly, it can possess you. That's why the tales about demonic possession; you get a Talented youngling or one who blooms late, who comes to power with no training—they go mad. Worst of all, they *know* they're going mad. It's bad—and you only hope you can save them before any real damage is done."

"Aye," Kasten agreed. "I suspect that's where the dragon's teeth tale comes from, too—which is why I told your man there to remind you of it. The analogy being that the younglings are the teeth, the trained mage is the dragon. What I'd like to know is what's to do about this? You can't take the younglings to the Academe—and *I* surely couldn't handle them!"

"No, they're too powerful," Martis agreed. "They need someone around to train them *and* keep them drained, until they've gotten control over their powers instead of having the powers control them. We have a possible solution, though. The Guild has given me a proposition, but I haven't had a chance to discuss it with Lyran yet." She craned her head around to look at him. "How would you like to be a father for the next half-year or so?"

"Me?" he replied, too startled to refer to himself in third person.

She nodded. "The Council wants them to have training, but feels that they would be best handled in a stable, homelike setting. But their blood-parents are frightened witless of them. But you— you stood up to them, you aren't afraid of them— and you're kind, love. You have a wonderful warm heart. And you know how I feel about youngsters. The Council feels that we would be the best parental surrogates they're ever likely to find. If you're willing, that is."

Lyran could only nod speechlessly.

"And they said," Martis continued with great

satisfaction in her voice, "that if you'd agree, they'd give you anything you wanted."

"Anything?"

"They didn't put any kind of limitation on it. They're worried; these are *very* Talented children. All five of the Councillors are convinced you and I are their only possible salvation."

Lyran tightened his arms around her. "Would they—would they give this one rank to equal a Masterclass mage?"

"Undoubtedly. You certainly qualify for Swordmaster—only Ben could better you, and he's a full Weaponsmaster. If you weren't an outlander, you'd *have* that rank already."

"Would they then allow this one to wed as he pleased?"

He felt Martis tense, and knew without asking why she had done so. She feared losing him so much—and feared that this was just exactly what was about to happen.

But they were interrupted before he could say anything.

"That and more!" said a voice from the door. It was the Chief Councillor, Dabrel, purple robes straining over his stomach. "Swordmaster Lyran, do you wish to be the young fool that I think you do?"

"If by that, the Mastermage asks if this one would wed the Master Sorceress Martis, then the Mastermage is undoubtedly correct," Lyran replied demurely, a smile straining at the corners of his mouth as he heard Martis gasp.

"Take her with our blessings, Swordmaster," the portly mage chuckled. "Maybe you'll be able to mellow that tongue of hers with your sweet temper!"

"Don't *I* get any say in this?" Martis spluttered.

"Assuredly." Lyran let her go, and putting both hands on her shoulders, turned so that she could face him. "Martis, *thena*, lady of my heart and Balance of my soul, would you deign to share your life with me?"

She looked deeply and soberly into his eyes.

"Do you mean that?" she whispered. "Do you really mean that?"

He nodded, slowly.

"Then—" she swallowed, and her eyes misted briefly. Then the sparkle of mischief that he loved came back to them, and she grinned. "Will you bloody well *stop* calling yourself 'this one' if I say yes?"

He sighed, and nodded again.

"Then that is an offer I will *definitely* not refuse!"

Bitch

by Marion Zimmer Bradley

Darkness falling in Old Gandrin, in an unfamiliar quarter of the city; Lythande, Pilgrim Adept of the Blue Star, alone, isolated, and abandoned, far from her usual haunts—insofar as she had usual haunts, or could count on anything to recur and be ordinary in her far from ordinary life. To add to the general dismalness of the night, a light rain was falling—not heavy but a drizzling persistence, not enough to soak anything, but enough to banish dryness, warmth, or comfort and imbue everything with a miserable and pervasive dampness throughout.

Although the streets of Old Gandrin were perhaps safer for an Adept of the Blue Star than for an average citizen, they could hardly be said to be altogether safe for anyone after dark, and Lythande had no more desire than anyone else to be attacked or robbed in the deserted fields in the graveyard district. She had come there considerably earlier in the day in search of certain herbs and ingredients for the making of spells; it was said to add to the efficacy of such ingredients that they grew or had been gathered in the shadow of the gallows.

Lythande was not altogether certain that she believed this; but if the clients of the magician believed it, she could hardly afford the luxury of flaunting this belief; after all, belief was a major ingredient that must be liberally stirred into every spell before it could work at all.

Around her stretched a series of barren open fields that had perhaps been last cultivated before the city walls were built; here and there the dim lights of occasional scattered dwellings in the rainy darkness. Even if the night had been clear, there would have been little moon; it was her business to know such things. The aforesaid gallows cast a long and wavering shadow almost to Lythande's very feet; there was no sign anywhere of light such as might have marked out an inn or any such place where one might find lodging. Beyond the gallows a broken field stretched, lumpy and barren with the uneven shapes of old and fallen gravestones. A deserted place, good perhaps for ghosts, but less salubrious for mortals; and Lythande, in spite of a life prolonged by magic to the span of three ordinary lifetimes, still counted herself among the living and mortal.

At this moment a shadow crossed her path and a not unfamiliar voice spoke: "Who goes there? Speak!"

"I am a minstrel and magician by the name of Lythande," she said, and in answer came the most unexpected of words:

"Greetings, fellow Pilgrim; what do you on this lonely road at this godforgotten hour?"

"If indeed there are gods, a question about which

I entertain certain doubts," Lythande observed calmly, "I would think it unlucky to call any place godforgotten in the fear that they might in fact forget it."

"Even if there be no gods," replied the newcomer, a dark shadow on the path, "I should consider it unlucky to say so, for fear that if they do in fact exist and I show bad manners by refusing to believe in them, they might retaliate by refusing to believe in me."

Lythande found the sound of that paradox sufficiently familiar to say, "Do I speak, then, to a fellow Pilgrim?"

"You do," replied the voice. "I am your fellow minstrel Rajene; we have debated these questions before this time in the courts of the Blue Star to the sound of the lute. Do I guess rightly that we should together seek shelter, if only against damp and ghosts, for the exchange of songs?"

"I am unfamiliar with these quarters," Lythande said. "And while I have not yet encountered a ghost here or elsewhere, I observe somewhat similar precautions about ghosts as you against gods touching their existence or nonexistence; in case I should have good reason for abandoning my disbelief."

Now in the darkness, Lythande could make out the lines of a voluminous mage-robe cut like her own, deeply hooded; and in the folds of the mage-robe's hood, the pale blue burning outline of a star like the one that glowed between her own brows. She said, "If you know of any shelter against this possibly god-infested and ghost-harboring quarter, I will follow you to it."

Rajene's voice was a strong and resonant baritone; far deeper than the mellow and sexless contralto of Lythande's own, though perhaps equally musical. Across the back where Lythande's lute was slung, Lythande could make out the outline of a *chitarrone*, an archaic but tuneful instrument almost as tall as the man who bore it. In fact, of all her fellow adepts of the Blue Star, there were few Lythande would have rather met on a dark night; for as far as she knew, she had no quarrel with Rajene, and when they were fellow apprentices in the Temple of the Star, they had been friends—or as near to friends as any magician could come to friendship. Which is to say that at the least, they were not enemies.

Lythande had had no true friends there; had dared have none; for alone among all the Pilgrim Adepts from one end of Time to the other, Lythande was a woman; alone and in disguise she had penetrated the secrets of the temple, and only after she bore the Blue Star between her brows had her disguise been exposed. She had paid the highest price ever for the power of a Pilgrim Adept; for when the truth was known, the Master of the Star had laid a doom upon her, thus:

"Be then, forever, what you have chosen to be," he said, "For on that day when your true sex shall be proclaimed aloud to any man save myself, on that day is your power at an end, and your immunity from your fellows."

So it had been since that day; a life of perpetual concealment, without relief; an eternal solitude, with none but brief and superficial companionship, such as she might now find for a time with Rajene.

And now, as if to add to the general bleakness

of the deserted and ghost-haunted quarter, the faint mizzling rain began to come down harder into the darkness, blotting out even the semblance of any ordinary night.

Lythande was not altogether sorry; the faint grizzling rain of the past hours would create discomfort, but added nothing to the safety of the darkness; this sudden downpour would send any enterprising footpad or cutpurse back to shelter, or if desperate, would make it less likely that an assailant would identify the victim as a Pilgrim Adept. No sane thief would attempt to rob a magician of that stature; but in this darkness and rain, they might not be deterred.

Rajene tugged the hood of his mage-robe tighter over his head, trying to rearrange the folds to protect the musical instrument.

"Let us seek shelter," he said urgently. "I have not visited these parts for many years—I forget quite how many; but if my memory still serves me at all, there was once an old dame who kept a kind of alehouse, and when her public-room was not too full, she would allow me to sleep on her floor by the fire. It was not the best shelter, but it was an inestimable improvement over the rain; and this is not such a night as I would willingly sleep under the stars—if there were any stars to sleep under, which there are not."

"Lead on," Lythande said briefly. "I follow."

This was better than she had hoped. She had little fear of women; and she had dwelt among the Adepts of the Blue Star for seven years of her apprenticeship without her true sex being even once suspected or exposed. A large public inn filled with men would have meant a night of endless vigilance; in the company of one fellow Pilgrim Adept and an old woman—and if Rajene's old acquaintance had been elderly in Rajene's early days as a magician, she must be truly venerable now—she would have little to fear.

She followed Rajene's shadowy form before her, with little light except the pallid glimmer of the Blue Star that shone faintly between her brows, and the similar gleam escaping from beneath Rajene's concealing hood.

She tried to protect her lute from the worst of the rain—not easy to do because the spell that kept it dry was a taxing one, and when she had concentrated on keeping up with Rajene in the darkness, she tended to lose sight of the spell. At worst it was more important that the lute be kept dry than that her own feet and body be sheltered from rain; they would dry without harm, and the lute would not.

After what seemed a long time of darkness and rain, stumbling on uneven ground broken with what might have been old sunken gravestones, Lythande made out the dim lights of a cottage—an old and tumbledown building with sagging stone walls and a door of planks so old, split, and broken that the firelight streamed out between them. Sheltering out of the wind (which came around the corner of the building with howling violence), Lythande hugged her mage-robe close to her shoulders and thought that even if this place was deserted and the haunt of ghosts or even ghouls, she would have shelter this night from the rain.

From inside came the sound of a cracked and quavering voice; then the door was pulled open from inside and a stooped old woman stood in the firelight. She was dressed in faded rags and tatters, a much-patched shawl over her bent shoulders being almost more patch than shawl, her face so wrinkled and drawn that Lythande, who was herself immensely old, could not even begin to guess her age.

"Dame Lura," cried Rajene, "I rejoice to see that you still dwell in this world! I have brought a friend to beg shelter at your fire this night. Had you no longer dwelled here, I was prepared to spend this wild night begging shelter of some poor ghost in his tomb!"

Dame Lura chuckled, a sound that seemed to Lythande so wild and humorless that it was hardly human.

"Ah, Rajene, my friend, there is better shelter than that for you here; even if this were no better than a tomb, I would deny shelter neither to the living nor the dead on such a night as this. Come inside; dry yourself by the fire there." She gestured them to the hearth, where a large rug covered the cold stone, and stretched out on the stone lay two large dogs, hairy and shaggy, sound asleep with their noses to the fire.

Rajene shoved one—the nearer dog, black and shaggy—with his foot, and the animal made a sleepy grumbling sound without waking, and scooted a little to one side to make room for Rajene to shed the mage-robe and hang it over a rickety stool that stood at the edge of the hearth-rug. After a moment, Lythande did the same, boosting another stool to the fireside and hauling off the half-drenched mage-robe. Rajene sat between the dogs, stretching his stockinged feet to the fire, and drew the *chitarrone* to himself, tuning the instrument to make certain it had taken no harm. Lythande pulled off her boots, stretching her narrow feet to the fire. The smaller of the two dogs, a tan and shaggy long-haired bitch, crowded against her, but the animal was warm and friendly, and after all, it had a better right to the fire than she did.

Dame Lura pulled a huge cauldron from its crane over the fire and asked, "May I offer ye some supper? And will ye play me a tune on yer lutes?"

"Pleasure," muttered Rajene, and began to play an old ballad of the countryside. Lythande discovered that the strings of her lute were soaked with the rain; but she had spare lengths of gut stowed in the many pockets of the mage-robe; she fumbled in them and set about mending and replacing the strings.

The old woman scooped a ladleful of stew into each of a couple of coarsely carved wood bowls and held one bowl out to Lythande. It smelled delicious, and Lythande, seeing that Rajene was looking into the fire and not at her, ventured a couple of bites. One of the many vows fencing the power of a Pilgrim Adept was that she might neither be seen to eat nor drink in the sight of any man; but the vows did not apply to women, and Rajene was not looking at her. She chose to apply the prohibition quite literally, and hastily, while Rajene was bent over his instrument and tuning it, she managed to get down a good part of the stew; though when he raised his eyes and asked her to play, she at once left off eating.

"No, you play; I am not familiar with the sound of the *chitarrone*," she replied. He seemed gratified by the request, and again bent his face over the lute so that Lythande managed to finish the stew. After that, Lythande played and sang, but soon began to feel sleepy close to the fire; covered herself with the mage-robe, which also covered the dogs; and tumbled quickly into sleep. Her last awareness was of the strong smell of wet dog hair, and of Rajene snoring on the rug beside her.

When she woke, she was aware of the firelight and silence; she looked up and saw no sign of Rajene, but only the big dog stretched out on the hearth. Then, about to stretch out, she looked at her hand and her hand was not there—only a hairy tan paw extended toward the fire. Something was wrong with her perspective; she seemed closer to the fire than before. She sprang up, trying to cry out, and heard only a long, lugubrious howl. At the sound the other dog sprang up, barking wildly; and above the dog's low, hairy forehead, she saw a pale gleam of blue in the shape of a star. She *recognized* the other dog; it was Rajene. And she herself had somehow been transformed into the bitch that had been lying beside her on the rug.

Dame Lura still crouched over her cauldron, muttering in some unknown language—or was it only that Lythande could no longer understand human speech? Lythande rushed in panic for the door, on all fours, followed by the other dog who was Rajene.

Outside, it had stopped raining; and by a curious distorted moonlight, she raced through the deserted lands; stumbling over gravestones, Rajene racing after her.

Transformed by sorcery; and since I have be-

come a bitch, Rajene will know I am a woman, she thought, and wondered why she was thinking about that; trapped in animal form, she could not even speak a spell to break the enchantment. Or was this the kind of spell that lasted only until sunrise or moonset? But why had nothing warned her of magic in action? The Blue Star should have warned her of the presence of sorcery. Yet in all justice she realized that the unaccustomed warmth after a cold soaking, the hot food, and her attempt to eat unobserved had taken her mind from any thought of hostile magic.

She wondered for a moment if Rajene had betrayed her. No, he himself was victim of the same magic; they had blundered together into the spell.

Rajene was still racing away in panic; Lythande tried to call out to him, but heard only a curious whining growl and desisted almost at once.

Can this be only a dream? Can it be that I am still lying before the fire in the witch's cottage, dreaming this? she wondered; but the chill of the graveyard was penetrating the pads on her paws, and there was no change in the dream-surroundings; so this was no dream, but some vicious sorcerous reality, and she—as well as Rajene—was trapped inside it.

Rajene—or rather, the dog in whose consciousness Rajene now dwelt—stopped his headlong rush, and turned back toward her, whining pitifully and circling around, barking softly. Then he stopped and whimpered, stretching himself out as if he were trying to crawl with shame into the very ground.

Lythande's thoughts were now wholly concerned

with the spell into which she had blundered; and how she could get out of this. There were magical herbs that grew in the shadow of the gallows; perhaps she could find one that would break the spell. The problem was that she had no particular belief in the efficacy of that kind of spell. Nevertheless, under these circumstances she found her disbelief eroding away; it evidently made a difference which side of the spell you were on.

She looked round, trying to orient herself from the peculiar perspective of a dog's vision; her eyesight was excellent, but everything seemed very high up and she was afraid of stumbling over the gravestones. The long shadow of the gallows still dominated the wasteland; and she went closer; she smelled the faint bitterness and found the herb for which she was looking, the threefold shiny leaf and pale berry, colorless by moonlight—although by normal day and in normal sight, it might have been pale green. She bent to nibble the herb; she knew from experience that it was faintly bitter, like most herbs; but when her sharp dog's teeth bruised the leaf, it was intense, nauseating, releasing a harsh, violent oil that flooded her with such sickness that she reflexively spat it out.

So much for that. Dogs didn't eat herbs—she should have remembered that. They sometimes ate grass when they were sick, but evidently sorcery did not qualify as an illness.

She tried to bite at the ordinary grass to take the taste of the herb out of her mouth; the grass tasted bland and coarse, like tasteless lettuce. What next? She recalled an ancient superstition; if she circled seven times clockwise round the gallows

. . . or was it counterclockwise? Well, she would try it seven times clockwise; and if that had no effect, she would try it seven times counterclockwise; and if *that* had no effect—well, she would have to think of something else.

But Rajene—to her amazement, she saw that the larger dog was bounding around the gallows and actually frisking his tail—had already thought of that. She followed, but nothing happened; as she began her eighth circumambulation of the gallows, she stopped and reversed the direction.

But nothing happened. *We could keep this up all night; dogs probably would.* She scowled—it distorted her vision oddly because her hairy forehead was at such an odd angle to her eyes—and flung herself down on the grass to think of any other possibility.

There must be something else that they could try. She turned about to look for Dame Lura's cottage. If she went back and confronted the hag, threatened to tear out her throat, the damnable hag would probably consent to take off her spell.

But she could not see the smallest glimmer of light from the witch's fire; she thought (but was not sure) that she could see the outline of the cottage, but it was entirely dark; the hag must have doused her fires and gone to bed, as if the enchanting of two wizards were just part of a good night's work. In a rage, Lythande thought, *Let me get my hands—my paws—on her, and if I don't make it the worst night's work she ever did, my name is not Lythande.*

Reversing her direction, she went bounding over uneven grass and gravestones toward the faraway dark outline of the cottage. Then she stopped; her acutely keen hearing in dog form sensed a movement on the grass not too far away; she stopped to allow Rajene to come up with her; she could hear him panting with his tongue hanging out.

The movement advanced, and a shadow loomed over her: a robed figure. A wizard? No, some kind of priest. His sacred staff was extended. Rajene jumped up and gripped the staff between his teeth. The priest cried out in surprise as the staff clattered to the gravestones. As Lythande touched it, she felt a shudder run through her limbs, and stretching, rose easily to her feet. The priest was gaping, reaching for his staff.

"A thousand pardons," Rajene said easily. "And as many thanks, for you have released us from an evil enchantment."

The priest gathered up his staff, with an exclamation of astonishment. Rajene was wearing a loose, whitish pajamalike garment; Lythande was dressed in leather tunic and breeches, and her feet were bare and cut on the loose stones and gravestones. Limping, she bowed to the priest, saying gravely, "Lythande thanks you, priest."

"Er—my pleasure to be of service," said the priest uneasily. "But tell me, how and when did all this happen? I did not know that this deserted quarter was subject to enchantments."

"Obviously we did not either," said Lythande, and Rajene added, "I thought I was visiting an old friend; I think now it must have been a ghost or evil fiend in her shape."

"An old friend living hereabouts?" asked the priest. "But my good man, no one dwells in this quarter."

"Dame Lura's cottage," Rajene said. "And I must return there—"

"But my good fellow," the priest began to argue, then, at Rajene's grim stare, subsided and followed him as he set out toward the outline of the cottage. "It is fortunate I came along; I was going out to greet the sun from that hill yonder. I visit this necropolis only once in a year, on the anniversary of the death of my old great-aunt; I come to say a prayer for her, for she was good to me in her own way, though I fear she was a wicked woman. This was that selfsame Dame Lura your companion claims to have seen—"

"*Claims* be damned," said Lythande. "Dame Lura sheltered us by her fire last night, and fed us with a stew that led to this enchantment."

"But my good man, that is simply impossible," said the priest, and followed them as they approached the dark line of the cottage. It was beginning to get light now, and she could clearly make out the familiar line of the odd peaked roof, though no light showed through the dilapidated planks of the door.

Rajene banged on the door, then shouted; silence. Then he shoved the door open.

Inside by the growing light, they could clearly see that the cabin was empty. No fire, no dogs, no rug where the dogs had lain; only bare stone flooring, and lying on the floor, two mage-robes, Lythande's lute, and the broken-stringed *chitarrone*.

"I suppose we should be glad for this," said Lythande, picking up the lute; she shrugged the mage-robe around her shoulders and felt less vulnerable, though the priest no more than any other man could have identified her lean, breastless figure as that of a woman. The spare strings of the lute were untouched in her pocket, the packet still sealed, yet she remembered mending and restringing the lute while she sat between the dogs on the hearth-rug.

Rajene, dressing slowly in his own mage-robe, looked angry, the Blue Star gleaming between his scowling brows. He went to the hearth, here the great cauldron still hung on its crane; inside the cauldron was cold and empty, yet Lythande could still in memory taste the stew she had eaten.

"I told you so," said the priest with a smug injured air. "Dame Lura died on yonder gallows fifty years ago this night."

Lythande turned her back on the empty cottage and began to walk swiftly away; she could clearly see now in the frost the footprints of two dogs, running this way, then abruptly her own human footprints and Rajene's coming to the cottage. After a moment, Rajene caught up with her.

"I gave the priest two silver pieces," he said. "Even though he disenchanted us by accident, I am grateful."

Lythande fumbled in her pockets and handed him a silver coin. "I will share the fee," she said.

"Even so, we were lucky," Rajene said. "We encountered no bitches. I have no sons; and if I did, they might well be sons of bitches; but I would prefer that they be so metaphorically rather than literally, if you take my meaning."

So he had not even noticed—or if he did, had thought Lythande assumed the other dog's shape out of default. "If I had had a son," Lythande said, trying to make her voice casual, "I would prefer that he be not a cur. Nevertheless, Rajene, I knew when we dwelt in the Temple of the Blue Star that you were a real son of a bitch. And now I can prove it."

The sun was coming up; Rajene looked at her and laughed. He said, "Let's find a tavern—and a pot of ale. I wish I knew what was in that stew."

Lythande said, "I'm sure we're better off not knowing."

"Let's go," said Rajene. "Last one to the city gates is a dirty dog."

"Right," said Lythande, thinking. *That's one expression I'll never use again.*

Of Honor and the Lion

by Jennifer Roberson

*I swear, I have never been so weary . . . of fight-
ing, of killing, of running, of walking; even, I
think, of living. But I do not dare do otherwise;
dying serves nothing, and no one, and I have
made promises.*

*One foot . . . one foot, step by step . . . one foot
in front of the other . . . keep walking . . . keep
running—stop for nothing and no one, not even
the child you carry—*

*I squeezed my eyes tight-shut. If only I could
rest—*

But I knew better.

*I had known better all along, but still I ig-
nored it, foolishly hoping and praying that for
once, if only for once, he would be man instead
of Mujhar.*

*Aloud, I told the child, "I should have known
better."*

*It kicked; did it agree? I clutched helplessly at
my belly.*

*"Not yet," I panted, tasting the dust of the
road. "Wait you only a little—at least till we
reach Mujhara . . . until we see the Lion . . ."*

I

The wolfhound bitch, asprawl on a rug near the firepit, wearily suckled nine squalling pups. Her ghost-gray mate paced the length of the hall to the marble dais, toenails clicking, tree-limb tail swinging. A man was seated there; more than a man, a king, embraced by the cavernous throne. He watched me, saying nothing. Absently fondling the wolfhound's ears, waiting for what I would say.

And so I said it: "No"

He stared, fingers arrested. Then he pushed the wolfhound away to give me his full attention.

"No," I said again.

Still he stared, gray eyes glittering. I have seen that look before; he meant me to give in. Often, too often, I did. This time I would not.

He sat very quietly in the throne all acrouch upon the dais. The Lion, Hale called it: the Lion Throne of Homana. My father was Mujhar. Worshiped by his subjects, served by the Cheysuli. By one in particular: Hale, liege man. Who, whenever he chooses, wears the guise of a fox.

So quietly he sat within the Lion's embrace, nothing at all astir, save gray, glittering eyes. Not the feral yellow of Hale's; my father is Homanan. He claims no Cheysuli blood.

Neither does his daughter. All she claims is a *Cheysuli*, who heats her Homanan blood.

Moving not at all, until he spoke my name. In a tone of subtle command, expecting me to give in as so many others give in, knowing nothing else but perfect service to the Mujhar.

"Lindir," he said.

Now I shook my head.

He moved then, but slightly, shifting forward a little, as if he feared the lion's mouth, obscenely agape above his head, would somehow swallow my words, warping the substance of what I said, meaning something else.

He would come to know I did not.

Candlelight glittered off gemstones and gold. It weighted fingers, banded brow, stretched from shoulder to shoulder. He had adorned himself for the feast at which he had planned to make the announcement.

Now I stole the chance, tarnishing pride with my defiance.

"You will," he told me gently. "The arrangements have been made."

"*Un*make them," I said. "I will not marry him."

There, the words were said. And plainly, he thought me mad. All he could do was gape, mimicking the lion. Unattractive on my father; his flesh was made for better things.

Color congested his face. Slowly, but it came, creeping in, ignoring his rank, shapechanging paternal sanguinity into sanguinary red.

His voice now was thickened, lacking customary timbre. "You are a term of the accord."

"I was never asked if I *wanted* to be a term."

Patent astonishment: "Why *should* you be asked?"

It was all I could do not to shout at him, though unsurprised by his reaction. And half expecting it; kings and fathers are accustomed to obedience in their children. Certainly mine was; I had always given it freely. But this time I could not.

Quietly, carefully, I drew in a breath, and answered. "Because I am not a cow, to be bred for milk at her owner's pleasure. I am not a mare, matched to the fastest stallion to produce fleeter offspring." I glanced briefly at the wolfhound bitch, sprawled on the rug with her pups. Then met his stare again, matching its intensity; I have my father's eyes. "Neither am I a bitch, suckling puppies twice a year whether I want to or not, having no choice in the matter." I lifted my head a little. "I am a woman . . . I am *Lindir*—I will not be anything else. Less *or* more."

Now he sat back in the Lion. I had, all unknowing, given him a weapon. And now he would use it. "Ah, but you *are* more," he said. "You are Lindir of Homana, daughter to Shaine the Mujhar. It gives you value, my girl, whether you like it or not."

The taste was sour on my tongue. "Value," I said in disgust. "Is that how I am judged?"

"Aye," he answered softly. "For the blood in your veins, my girl, and the children you will bear."

Frankness, at least; no more prevarication. The truth was disconcerting, though not really a surprise. It was just that my father had never said such before, to me, couching his words in kindness and courtesy, avoiding things of substance.

"So," I said in bitterness, "when you did not get a son on my mother, you decided to use me. One day, some day, when I was grown . . . is that why you have not let me marry before now?" I fought down rising anger. Not because I had not wed before now, but because of the requisites that govern girls of royal birth. "Men have asked, I know: princes, and kings for their sons. As you say, I am Shaine's daughter . . . surely *someone* wanted me."

"Ellas, Erinn and Caledon," he agreed. "And I said no to all of them, saving you for something more."

The word was ash in my mouth. "Solinde," I said flatly.

"Ellic," he confirmed. "Bellam's only son, and heir to everything."

Loss of control would accomplish nothing. I bit back frustration and helplessness, taking solace in secret knowledge. I had a weapon, too, though I hoped I would not be forced to use it.

"Did Bellam ask? Or did you offer?" I paused. "Who *made* me one of the terms?"

"It is often done," he said. "Sons and daughters are wed to insure alliances."

So, he had offered; it did make a difference. To my actions, as well as my pride. Quietly, I said, "I have always been an obedient daughter—"

"Until now."

"—until now." I drew in a breath for patience. "But as it is I who am most inconvenienced by this marriage, I think—"

"*I* think you are a spoiled, selfish bitch."

It stopped me short with its brutal bluntness, as he meant it to. Shocked into silence, all I could do was stare. He had never spoken so to me, *never*, only to those who crossed him, who threatened pride and authority; both were absolute. Too stunned to breathe, to speak, to cry, I stood completely still. Feeling my flesh turn cold. Knowing I would lose.

My father rose. He stood before the Lion, weighted with gold and gems and the manifest power of a king. He explained to me my place, then cruelly put me in it.

"Ellic of Solinde," he began coldly, "is of an age with you, which is more than most girls get when war plays matchmaker. He is battle-proved. He is sound of limb and soul. He has six bastards to credit his manhood." Behind the line of graying dark beard, I could see the set of his mouth. Hard and cold and unyielding. "He is all of that, Lindir, as well as heir to the throne of Solinde. And you *will* be his queen."

I threw his pride back at him. "He is the son of the enemy!"

"Solinde and Homana are at peace." His tone was deceptively gentle. "No more are we enemies, Lindir, after centuries of warfare. A peace has been made at last . . . *and you are one of the terms!*"

He might as well have been the Lion, the roar reverberated so. As before, I could only stare. My lips were very dry, but I did not dare to wet them.

His shout had dissipated. He spoke very softly again, but with no less intensity. "I have given you everything, and you have taken freely. Now it is your turn to give."

I hated myself for crying. More than I hated him. But not as I hated Ellic. "I do not desire to wed him—"

"—no more than he, you," he told me curtly. "Ah, I see you are shocked." Briefly, he smiled. "Thinking only of yourself, Lindir, you neglected to think of Ellic. He wants this marriage no more than you. He has been suckled on war just as you have, and on hatred for the enemy; his has been Homana. Do you expect Bellam's Solindish son to desire Shaine's Homanan daughter any more than she desires him?" He shook his head slowly. "He

108

is as bound as you are, but he understands his duty. He will bear his burden."

I struggled to speak clearly, knowing anger or tears or desperation would make him ashamed of me. A man ashamed of his daughter will turn away, not listen. "And I Ellic's children?"

His mouth was very taut. "More than your mother bore me."

It was, I knew, a bone of contention between them, and had been for years. No son for Homana, only a single daughter. And she was not enough. The Lion demanded a male.

I drew in a very deep breath. "Have I no say at all?"

"You have had it already." Then his tone softened. "Lindir, surely you understand—I must have an heir. Your mother will bear me none; the Lion is dry of sons." His expression, too, had softened. I saw appeal in it now. He wanted understanding. He desired my compassion for the man who had no sons. "Bear Ellic two sons, or even three, then give one of them to me. Give one of them to the Lion; Homana has need of a prince."

I looked him straight in the eye. I summoned all my strength, all my control; hid away humiliation. "Do you want me to beg?" I asked.

It shocked him deeply. It stripped away all his magnificence and left him with deathmask and shroud.

And then, abruptly, *alive*, he came down from the Lion, down from the dais, and caught me, grasping my arms, holding me tightly, gripping with all his strength.

"You will beg for nothing!" he cried. "Nothing. Never. From no one. Do you hear? Do you hear?

You are my daughter, *my daughter*, the flesh and blood of kings and queens—" He broke it off abruptly, as stunned as I was by his vehemence, but it did not stop him. Not entirely. He took his hands from me only; held me in place with ferocious pride. "You will beg for *nothing*."

Numbly, I nodded. "I understand, my lord."

He heard what he expected, what I intended him to hear, nothing more. Nothing of what I felt. "Then I dismiss you, Lindir, to your chambers, where you may be attired as befits a princess on her betrothal day." He smiled, tracing back from my face a fallen strand of rose-gold hair. "Ellic will be astounded."

I took my leave and departed. Behind me, he spoke to the wolfhound. More gently than to me.

The child was heavy within me. Uneasily, it shifted, disturbed by my activity, my bid for a final rescue. Nothing else was left. No one else was left, save the man who was my father; who was death as well as life, offering both in abundance.

The child. Always the child, once nothing more than a word, now the future of a realm, the future of a race, and neither of them the same.

Kicking, twisting, shifting, protesting my exertions. I hugged my swollen belly, trying to soothe the child, promising relief, bribing it with lies.

All in the name of pride. In the name of injured honor.

I nearly laughed aloud, still hugging my too-large belly. "Pride," I said to the child. "Pride and honor. More powerful than magic—more en-

during than love—more destructive than weapons . . . and I think they will kill us both."

In answer, the child kicked. It nearly brought me down. I laughed raggedly, wiped sweat out of my eyes, considered what they would say; the heir of the Lion brought into the world in the heat and dust of the road? No, it would not do.

Gods, but my back hurt. "Not so far," I told it gently, stroking my squirming belly. "I promise, not so far . . . you have only to wait a little."

But it had waited nine months. Now it demanded freedom.

If I died, the child died. If it died, Homana died. Homana and the Cheysuli.

I staggered down the road, making promises to the child. Promises to a dead man: I will give the Lion a child.

II

In my chambers, where my father had sent me, I dismissed the women who had come to dress me as befits a princess. Startled, they stared, but went, knowing better than to ask questions. I shut the door on them all.

And as I had known he would, he came in through the antechamber. With him was his fox.

An honored, honorable man, warrior-born and bred, sworn to serve my father. And so he had, for years. For all the years of my life: eighteen of them.

He had a wife, Raissa; *cheysula* in the Old Tongue. He had Finn, a son of his own, and a foster-son, Duncan, born to his wife's first husband. He had a pavilion in the Keep, where the Cheysuli lived. But he also had a home here in

Homana-Mujhar, my father's palace; a man divided, serving his lord and his race by performing an ancient custom sacred to his people. Liege man to the Mujhar. Father, brother, son; indistinguishable and distinct.

And I knew, looking at Hale, that could my father do it, he would leave Homana to him.

But the Homanans would never accept it. He was Cheysuli: shapechanger: a man who becomes a fox at will, with an animal's habits and appetites. More yet than that: a man born of the race that had once ruled Homana, that had tamed a wild land, that had the blessing of the gods. Children of the gods; it was what *Cheysuli* meant.

Once purely Cheysuli, Homana was now Homanan, because the Cheysuli had stepped aside, forsaking the Lion freely, giving it over to the Homanans as a gesture of good faith, of proof that their sorcery was not evil; that they were a benevolent race. Serving the new aristocracy with all the honor they could offer.

For centuries they had served. Homana was now my father's, but with no son to succeed him.

Instead, he would name a grandson born of his Homanan daughter's loins, bred of Solindish Ellic.

I looked at Hale. "You know him as well as I—" But I broke it off, shrugged, tried to sound unconcerned. "Better by far than I; you have known him longer."

"Aye," he said gently. "Since before you were born."

Helplessly, I asked, "How did it come to this? How did it come to *this*?"

"A man and a woman are but children of the gods." A Cheysuli saying, though he quoted it in

Homanan. And then he quoted in the Old Tongue, in lyrical Cheysuli, making a fluid, scooping gesture that left his right hand palm-up with fingers spread. *"Tahlmorra lujhala mei wiccan, cheysu."*

I knew it so well: The fate of a man rests always within the hands of the gods.

Abruptly, I was angry. "Will you do nothing but mouth such things? What good are they to me? What good are they to Shaine's daughter, who must wed the enemy to provide *two* realms with sons for their thrones?" Tears ran down my face; before him, I could cry. "Is it so easy for you? Will you stand beside my father and say nothing as I am bartered away? As I am *sold* to Solinde: a term of the accord."

A muscle ticked beside one eye. A distinctly yellow eye, feral as a wolf's.

"He must have told you," I said. "Surely my father told you. You are his liege man; he tells you everything." Then my breath ran ragged. "You were there," I said numbly. "You were there, were you not, when my father offered me? To Bellam. To his son. To Solinde, as a term . . . you were there—you *must* have been—you are always with him in Council—" Now I could hardly speak, shivering in shock. "Was it you who *suggested* it?"

The light was fierce in his eyes. "Do you think," he said coldly, "that I would give up my children and *cheysula* for a woman I would suggest be bartered away?"

"Give up—" I echoed.

The anger peeled away, showing the nakedness of his need; Hale, who said so little. Who showed so little of himself, resolved to being a shadow to his lord in everything. Quiet, unobtrusive, even in emotions; a proper liege man.

Who loved his lord's daughter.

And a man who knew better.

They are a proud, prickly race, bound by honor codes more stringent than any I have known. Loyal, steadfast, dangerously single-minded when it comes to serving sovereign. But more so yet when it comes to serving their *tahlmorra*, their eternal destiny, the fate that rules their souls. Bound by ancient gods and self-imposed honor codes, they are not like other men.

Hale was like no one else. He had never been, for me.

But until this moment, I had not quite known what I was to him.

"After what we have shared," I said, "do you think I can marry Ellic?"

Again the muscle ticked. "No more than I can go back to the Keep."

I could not believe he meant it. Not Hale. Not the loyal liege man, sworn to a blood-oath. I must have misunderstood him, or read into his statement the thing I most wanted to hear.

Carefully, I said, "It is easier for you. You have said it before: in the clans, a warrior may take *cheysula* and *meijha*—wife and light woman— while giving honor to them both."

His tone was very steady. "Raissa bore me a son. I owe Finn more time, and Duncan, though he needs less of me." His mouth hooked down a little, but in wry affection. "Duncan needs no one but himself, I think, being self-possessed for a boy . . . but Finn—" he sighed a little, "—Finn will need more than most."

Aye, I had misheard him. I had hoped too high.

I drew in a painful breath. "You, of all people, understand what it is to serve, sacrificing personal desires in the name of a greater thing. But I lack your strength. All I want to do is run."

"And give up your heritage?"

"My heritage is myself." Bitterness crept in. "My father bequeathed me stubbornness, if little else, and determination. Spoiled, selfish bitch, he called me; well, perhaps I am. But I will not marry Ellic. I will not bear my sons for Solinde."

His voice was very quiet. "What of for the Lion?"

If fanned my anger again. "Am I to be nothing more than a broodmare, then, parceling out my sons? One to Solinde, one to Homana—"

"—one to the Cheysuli." Now he moved, for the first time since he had entered, coming to me, to take my hands and hold them, but doing no more than that. "Lindir, we are all governed by the gods. Cheysuli, Homanan, Mujhar and liege man . . . even the Mujhar's daughter. You say you will give no children to Homana, but I say you will. I have it on good authority."

"The prophecy." I said it without heat, though I think he knew what I felt. I am not overfond of the prophecy, a distinctly Cheysuli thing, born of Homana's ancestors, ruling today's descendants. The prophecy claimed one day a man of all blood would unite, in peace, four warring realms and two magical races. It foretold the coming of the Firstborn, Homana reborn again in the blood of the ancestors, united in one man. A man with power incarnate: shapechanger, healer, sorcerer, all dedicated to good. "Your prophecy says *my* son will rule?"

"A child of your loins will beget the first Cheysuli Mujhar in nearly four hundred years."

"And Ellic's," I said bitterly.

His hands tightened on mine. "Ellic is not Cheysuli."

"No, no, of course not," I agreed impatiently, "but what does it matter? If I am wed to him and I bear him a son, your prophecy is proved right."

"Is it?" Hale smiled. "I think it is more likely you will bear a Cheysuli child."

"Oh?" I arched my brows. "And do you intend to come with me to Solinde, to *serve* me there?" Purposely, I was crude. "I think it might discompose my husband."

Now he let go of me. I saw in his eyes the feral glint usually masked by civility. But a Cheysuli is not quite human, no matter how human his shape. He *thinks* differently, no matter how human his words.

His tone was intense. "What did you tell your *jehan*?"

"That I would not marry Ellic."

"And did he use his wiles to change your mind?"

I smiled, a little. He knows my father so well, unsurprised by anything. There was irony in his tone, compounding the bitterness.

I shrugged. "You know him. You know me. Whom do you think won?"

For the first time, Hale grinned. Incongruous on his predator's face, but fitting all the same. He lit up my chamber. He lit up my heart. He set my world ablaze.

"Shaine thinks *he* has won; you would make certain of that, if you intended to thwart him still. I know *you*, Lindir."

Laughing, I nodded. "I left him with that impression."

"And what is the truth of the matter?"

The laughter spilled away. I had asked the question often, of myself; as often had answered it. And now I answered him. "I will have to go away. I would sooner live the life of a croftwife in Homana than the life of a queen in Solinde."

"Oh?" Black brows rose. "You have a crofter in mind?"

I laughed again into his face, suddenly emboldened by my decision. The weight was gone from my shoulders; I had said what I would do. "My father's arms-master has always been very kind to me. Torrin has a brother whose croft is not so far from the border between Homana and Ellas. I could go there, and stay, until I decided my next step. My father would never suspect Torrin, nor would he think such a thing of me."

His expression was serious. "Better yet," he said, "come into the forests with me."

Oh gods, how I had hoped— "But you cannot," I told him. "You are liege man to the Mujhar. What of your honor, what of your oath . . . what of children and *cheysula*?" Even as I asked it, I was aware of duality. I wanted so badly for Hale to take me from Homana-Mujhar, from my father's authority, so I could live with him in freedom. But I knew, in doing it, he would abdicate half of his soul; Cheysuli oaths are binding. He would abjure his honor.

He did not look away. "An oath is binding so long as it serves the prophecy. This one no longer does."

I stared. "Are you saying this was *meant*? That

one day—someday, somehow, regardless of everything else—I would bear a child to you?"

"A child for the Lion, who will beget a Cheysuli Mujhar."

Suspicion was a serpent. "You are more honorable than any man I know, even other Cheysuli . . . the prophecy, to you, is more binding, I believe, than even the link with your *lir.*" I glanced at the vixen, Tara, sitting so patiently at Hale's side. It was all I could do to look back, to see the beloved face. Gods, but it hurt. "Then there is nothing at all between us save your service to your gods."

His mouth was taut and grim. "Honorable?" he asked. "I have lain with my liege's daughter, winning from her that which is due her *cheysul.*" Relentlessly, he went on. "I have left my woman and my children, my Keep, my clan, in the name of what is between us." His eyes were very fierce. "If that is not enough for you, you are not worth the sacrifice."

Gods, I wanted to be. I wanted to be worthy of *him.*

"How will we go?" I asked.

"I will be a fox." He smiled. "You shall be a servant."

Laggardly, I stirred. "I will require proper clothing; nothing I have will suit."

"Already done," he told me, and with that he sealed our fates as he sealed the fate of Homana.

I knew the guard no more than he knew me. He was young, younger than I, and shocked to see a woman so far gone with child demanding he open the gate, to be let into Homana-Mujhar.

"Lady," he said gently, so courteous, so kind; seeing my distress, my distended abdomen, "Lady, I beg you, go back where you came from; there is no one for you here."

I knew what he was thinking: that I intended to claim my child the Mujhar's, in hopes of gaining a coin, a gem, a place in Homana-Mujhar. It nearly made me laugh. I might have laughed, too, had I dared unlock teeth from bleeding lips.

Into his hand I put Hale's golden earring, shaped in the form of a fox.

His eyes widened. No woman desiring something of the Mujhar offered such a thing; now he was confused. "Lady—" he began.

"Show him," I said tautly. "Show the Mujhar." It was all I could manage, now, having come so far down the road.

He went. He came back. With him were others, including Torrin, my father's armsmaster, who had always been kind to me. To whose brother I would have fled, had Hale not taken me.

Through my pain, I smiled. "He wanted a child from me, a son for the Lion, though admittedly he might have preferred a different sire." I wanted to laugh, but could not. I drew in a deep, shaking breath, aware of hands reaching out, steadying, gently urging me onward, toward the rose-red palace. "Well, now he will have it." Blackness loomed so near. "Is my mother here?"

It was Torrin who answered quietly and gently into the sudden silence. "No, lady," he said. "Your mother died within a year of your departure, of a wasting disease."

I caught my breath on a contraction. "But—

119

Homana has a queen. I have heard it said—" I tried to stifle a cry as they led me forward. "I have heard—"

"Lorsilla," Torrin told me gently. "The Mujhar's second wife."

Second wife. "How long?"

"Nearly seven years."

"Wasted no time, did he?" Bitterly I looked at Torrin, quiet, competent Torrin, whose face was ashen with shock. "But no son, has he? That I would have heard."

"No son," he told me. "The Queen of Homana is barren, having borne a boy who died in childbirth."

I laughed aloud as they held me. And as I laughed I felt the waters break and gush down my thighs, soaking my homespun trews. Man's clothes I wore. No more the Lady Lindir.

"Gods," someone whispered, "she will birth the child here—"

"No," Torrin said, "she will birth it where she should. In her own chambers, beneath her own roof."

"The sky is my roof—" I mumbled. "—for eight years, my roof, with Hale at my hearth—"

Torrin scooped me up. "Your roof is here, Lindir. In the House of the Lion."

In my child's house.

III

In huddled shadows, we watched the sun go down. He said nothing, being locked away within himself, stroking his *lir* instead of me; was he wishing himself back? Did he regret what he had done, leaving kin, clan and king for the sake of a Homanan woman?

No. More than just for that; for the sake of Homana herself, and the Cheysuli race.

"He will be angry," I said.

Hale bestirred himself, setting aside the fox from his lap and reaching out instead to touch a lock of my hair, fallen over one shoulder.

"Angry," he agreed, "and hurt very deeply. It is a wound that will not entirely heal, not ever; we have done the unthinkable."

I moved closer to him, pressing against the flesh of his bare arm. Through my cloak, my tunicked overblouse, I felt the hard, carved metal of his *lir*-band, solid gold, clasped about his arm above the elbow. He wore another on his right, and an earring in his left lobe, all shaped to look like his vixen. Gold, heavy gold, bright Cheysuli gold, a symbol of the *lir*-bond; of a powerful, unflagging pride.

I touched one long-fingered hand, threading mine through his. "Had I gone without you, he would have sent you to find me."

Fallen hair, sweeping forward as he bent his head, shielded most of his face. In profile, I saw wide brow, straight nose, pronounced cheekbones, clean jaw, all carved by a master's hand. Bronze of skin, black of hair, eerily yellow of eyes. They are a handsome race, the Cheysuli, shaped of glorious angularities and smooth, taut skin. And an economy of motion that makes every movement count.

"To find you, to bring you back." His tone was crisp; he was still liege man, in his heart. If he could no longer serve his Mujhar, he would serve the Mujhar's daughter.

"And?"

"To give you over to punishment, for wanting a Cheysuli instead of Solindish Ellic." He lifted his head, looked at me; there was acknowledgment in his eyes, of what we had done, the two of us, and what would become of us both in the face of my father's wrath. "It might have been better had you gone to Torrin's brother. Sent, it would have made more sense . . . I could have simply disappeared, and you, and they would say evil had befallen us, instead of making up stories." He shook his head once, mouth crimped hard; he blamed himself only, giving me no portion. "I meant to say so, in your chamber, but there you were, afire from anger and anguish, afraid of what might happen, and I could not. All I could think to do was take you out of there with me, admittedly in disguise, but at least not separated. Not torn apart, as Shaine would have done, once he had seen what was between us."

"What will he do?" I asked.

"Send men to find us, to *take* us . . . to bring us back to Homana-Mujhar."

"What then?"

The muscles of his arm shifted beneath my hand, tightening, knotting, upstanding beneath his flesh. "He will send you to Solinde, if Ellic will take you still. Me he will dismiss." His eyes were fixed distances. "And I will be *kin-wrecked*, left with no one . . . no clan, no links to anyone save my *lir*, not even *cheysula* and children."

I drew in a painful breath, knowing he had lost far more than I had ever known. "But—you are without them now. No clan. No children, and no *cheysula*."

He turned his head. He touched me, stroking the line of my jaw, threading fingers through my hair. "With you, I have enough."

With him, I thought, I had everything.

The child would not be born. Having tasted the promise of life without a womb, it turned back, refusing, clinging to what it knew.

I opened my mouth and screamed.

"Gods," someone blurted, "the child will be the death of her."

Someone else answered. All women now, here; no men, who would profane the labor with ignorance. "So long as it is born, so long as it is a boy, the dying does not matter. So the Mujhar has said."

Gods, he hates me so. But a practical man, my father; he needed a boy for the Lion, and if I gave him one he would gladly accept it. Perhaps he would even love me again, for giving him his heir.

The first voice sounded appalled. "You wish the lady dead?"

"She started a war," the other said. "Ended peace with Solinde, and began the war again."

"But I heard the shapechanBr stole her for himself, that the lady had no choice. She was compelled, they say, through the force of his sorcery."

The second voice was grim, unrelenting, contemptuous. "They say what they are told."

I knew what my father told them. What he took pains to tell, so as to soothe his wounded pride and repair his battered honor. Lies, all of them. Every one, told again and again, with embellishment, to justify what he did in the name of his vanished daughter.

One: that Hale had stolen me.

Two: that the Cheysuli had cursed the House of Homana, depriving it of sons.

Three: that each and every Cheysuli worked to throw down the House of Homana, to steal the Lion for themselves.

Qu'mahlin, Hale called it. The annihilation of a race. The expunging of a people from the land they had made out of what their gods had given them, as ours had given us.

Exiles in their own land. Prey of the man they once had served with a perfect loyalty.

My father was slaughtering the Cheysuli. Every year, every month, every day. As many as he could find, indiscriminate of age or gender. He sent men out to kill them, and that is what they did.

Once, overcome, I had told Hale it was all because of me. That I was to blame for the deaths, and all the hatred.

He had told me no: Because of the prophecy. That we were merely tools.

I opened my mouth and screamed.

IV

They came upon us without warning, slicing the air with swords. Mounted on plunging horses, clad in Mujharan livery. My father's men, of course; a few had found us at last.

One of the men wore a crimson captain's baldric slashed across his chest. He saw us, cursed us, called us spawn of demons, as bad as the

Ihlini. And then he looked, and then he *saw* us, and realized who he had.

"By the gods!" he cried. "The traitor and his whore!"

Whore, was I? And Hale named a traitor? Neither. *Never.*

Cursing the captain in terms as elaborate as his own, I thrust myself from the underbrush and leaped to catch the horse's bit. I know something of horses; I yanked down on the shanks, then slammed my fisted free hand into his soft muzzle as hard as I could.

"Lindir!" It was Hale, reaching for me, catching an arm and jerking me away, nearly off my feet. I was pushed, ungently, back into the brush, back into the trees. "Run," he told me curtly, as the others began to gather.

"What of—"

"*Run.*"

I ran, but not far, only far enough to put myself beyond the sword's reach. I crouched down in underbrush, clawing thorns away, tearing flesh and not caring, thinking only of Hale.

His *lir* was a rusty blur, yapping, snapping, nipping at fetlocks to make the horses dance, keeping the swords at bay. I saw Hale, still in human form, jerk free and throw his knife. I saw it flash and fly home, buried in crimson baldric. No more would my father's captain call either of us names.

But there remained six of them, and Hale's knife was gone. His warbow was on the ground, and quiver; we had stopped to eat, to sleep, to lose our cares in one another, if only for a moment. Now we might lose our lives.

I scrabbled forward, crabbing across the ground, unmindful of nettles and briars, pausing once only to tear my hair free of thorns. And then I had it, Hale's bow, and the quiver full of arrows.

Gods, they will kill him—

I nocked and loosed the arrow, feeling the pull of the bow, the tremendous power, so at odds with its compact appearance. It was made so purposely.

One man tumbled from his horse, crying out in shock. The fletching stood up from his chest as the sword fell from his hand.

I nocked and loosed again.

Seven men, then six, not only five . . . four converged on Hale. I nocked, steadied, prepared to shoot, but none of the targets was still. And Hale was in their midst.

Abruptly, he was not. Not the Hale I knew. No longer a man but animal; beast, some would say.

It makes me queasy, the blurring, the void, the absence of substance in place of a man. I blinked, holding the bowstring much too tightly for accuracy. Hale had tried and tried to break the habit, but it was too firmly ingrained. I had grown up seeing the shapechange, but the emptiness always made me ill.

That a man can reshape himself—

My father's guardsmen were young, those who remained. Too young to recall the days when Cheysuli walked the streets of Mujhara freely, and the halls of Homana-Mujhara. Too young to recall that in addition to the shapechange, Cheysuli also could heal. Certainly too young to have witnessed a warrior trading human for animal, losing nothing of his humanity, his awareness, merely putting on a new shape as a man puts on new boots.

Old enough only to know that Cheysuli were worth the killing, because that is what they were told.

Much too young. They looked at Hale the man; at Hale now the animal. They looked at him and screamed.

Two foxes laced the horses' legs like embroidery, yapping, snapping, nipping. Driving the mounts into a frenzy, kicking, squealing, hopping, trying to rid themselves of tenacious irritation. And the men, still astride their horses, found it impossible to put a sword into either fox, for fear of striking fellow guardsman or plunging mount.

"Run," I muttered, "*run*—"

And so they did, the two of them, having driven the horses half mad. Two ruddy foxes, streaking through the brush, black-tipped brushes bobbing behind them as they ran.

My turn now.

With exceeding care, I nocked each successive arrow. One by one I took them down. One by one they died.

"Traitor?" I cried. "Whore? Better than any of you? *Better than my father*—"

Hale's hand was on my shoulder, a human hand, with human empathy. He took the warbow, the arrows, then closed my mouth with gentle fingers. "They were doing what they were told."

"To *murder* us, and others—?"

"That is Shaine's guilt, not theirs." His face was streaked with blood. Horse's, I wondered, or man's? "You must recall, Lindir, their honor depends upon an abiding obedience. And the welfare of Homana."

I scooped tangled hair from my face. "They might have killed us both."

"No. The child is not yet born."

"The *child!*" I cried, half-sobbing. "Always the child, with you! Have you forgotten, then? I have miscarried two of them already . . . this one, too, perhaps. What then, Hale? What then of the Cheysuli? What then of the Lion?"

"The child will be born. If not this one, another."

"How many more?" I cried. "How many nights of pain and grief, pouring out your half-formed seed onto the ground, the thirsty Homanan earth, crying out for blood?" I was shaking now, and crying, released from the requirements of survival into a reaction that stripped me of my dignity, but not of humanity. "How much longer, Hale? Nearly eight years now . . . how much longer will it continue?"

"Until it stops," he said, and turned me toward the deeper forest. "And it may, sooner than you think . . . Shaine has more than shapechangers to think about. Now he has Ihlini."

A ripple ran through my flesh. "Tynstar has joined Bellam?"

"Tynstar joins no one. He uses those he requires . . . for the moment, it is Bellam. And Solinde will pay the price." His tone was grim. "One day. When Bellam is not looking."

"And my father?" I asked.

"Of a certainty."

I thought of my father. I thought of Bellam. But mostly I thought of Tynstar, called the Ihlini, and all the others like him. The man born of a race of sorcerers who serve Asar-Suti, the god who made and dwells in darkness, who rules the nether world.

I shivered. Once, Homana could have withstood Ihlini sorcery, for in the Cheysuli she had a share of her own. Now, without them, there was nothing but men to halt Tynstar's magic.

And I knew men were not enough.

"It will not be born," someone said. "The child refuses."

In my extremity, it was all I could do to whisper. "Perhaps because it knows it will find no welcome in the house or heart of its grandsire."

Through slitted, greasy lashes I saw them, the women, exchanging glances of shock, guilt, acknowledgment. I knew none of them; it had been eight years since I had left Homana-Mujhar, and my father saw fit to deny me anyone I might feel comfortable with. Even as I bore the child who might well become the heir to Homana, he desired to punish me.

If I bore it.

If I lived to bear it.

"Hale," I said aloud. "If Hale were here—" But I broke it off, knowing what the outraged gasps portended. They would go and tell my father that even now I called out for the shapechanger who had freely broken his oath, that I desired the traitor even in extremity. In eight years my father had pulled a blanket over the eyes of his subjects, blinding them all, so that new generations would consider the Cheysuli evil, and kill them with impunity.

*Older people would know better. Men like
Torrin, a Mujhar's man, yet fair, who knew Hale
nearly as well as I, or had; who knew me better.
Women like my mother, who had given thanks
to the gods that a man like Hale could keep her
small daughter safe against all odds . . . and
still did, though now the mother was dead and
the daughter no longer small.*

*But the others would not admit it, if they knew.
Blind obedience to the Mujhar, shutting away
the light from their minds.*

*My lord Mujhar, you are a fool . . . and, I
think, a madman—*

V

Hale's face was ashen. I said his name once,
twice, thrice, but he ignored me. He had gone
beyond me into grief, into shock so binding that
nothing so tame as his *meijha* calling his name
would touch him. For no matter how much a warrior
loved his woman, the *lir*-bond took precedence.

And now that bond was broken.

"Tynstar," he said emptily. "Tynstar and his
godfire, the blood of Asar-Suti."

It set the hairs to rising on my arms. There is
much I do not know of Ihlini, save they, like my
father, desire the destruction of the Cheysuli. But
godfire I do know, the cold, purple fire that eats
through flesh and bone, even through hardest
stone. The blood of Asar-Suti, issuing from the
netherworld.

Tynstar had barely touched Tara. Caressed, she
was nearly consumed.

There was little left of the *lir* except a parody.

Legs were curled obscenely, crisped into twisted sinew. Fur was blackened, charred, stinking of sorcery; even I could smell it. The Ihlini had killed Hale's *lir* and stripped me of my warrior.

I touched his arm gently. "Hale—if we stay, Tynstar will find us as well."

He seemed not to see Tara as she was now. He seemed not to see me. Only the loss of his heart, his soul, his life.

His voice belonged to someone else. "You know the price, Lindir."

Aye, I did. A warrior deprived of his *lir* by death was constrained by custom to leave clan, kin, life; to give himself over to an obscene rite called the death-ritual. Because, I had been told, a warrior without a *lir* was only half a man, having no magic, no shapechange, doomed to a slow, certain madness. That, no Cheysuli would countenance. And so warriors like Hale, lacking a *lir*, walked out of life into death, however it happened to take them.

"If we stay here—"

"Then go." His eyes were oddly unfocused. Clearly, he was in pain. More than grief and anguish, but also pain of body. Not being Cheysuli, I could not begin to comprehend. But I saw the agony in his eyes, the emptiness of his soul. He was not the Hale I knew.

"Will you let Tynstar kill us as well?" I set broken nails into his flesh and pulled, trying to force him up, to run, to *go*. "Gods, Hale, think of something more than Tara's death . . . think of your *child*, who may inherit the Lion, or sire the child who will—"

He threw me off easily. "Go," he said. "Run, then; save yourself, and the child. But I can do nothing more."

"Except die?" I wanted to strike him, to batter down his unexpected implacability. "Are you a fool, to throw away life because Tynstar has killed your *lir*? I know what you have said about the death-ritual, but surely it is more myth than truth." Frenziedly, I caught at his hand. "After taking me out of Homana-Mujhar to live like a fugitive for eight years, killing to stay alive, you now refuse responsibility? You tell me to go and turn your back—Hale, it is *your child* I carry! Are you blind to that? To what your prophecy demands?"

He spun faster than I could have predicted, catching my wrists and holding them against his chest, trapping me easily. "Lindir!" he cried. "Nowhere in the prophecy does it say I live to see the child!"

I gaped at him. "And you will let *that* make your decision?" Bitterly, I shook my head. "You fool, you yourself have said not all of the prophecy was recovered, that bits and pieces are missing . . . without full knowledge of what the gods intend, you are sentencing yourself to death." I tried to twist free, could not. "I am sorry Tara's dead, but it does not have to mean *you* must die, too! Gods, Hale—"

And abruptly, he was in my mind, shutting off my thoughts, my words, my feelings, shunting all of them aside to replace them with his own. It is yet a third gift of the Cheysuli—the shapechange, healing, compulsion—and now he used it against me.

"You will sleep," he said. "For an hour, two . . .

by then it will be over. By then Tynstar will be dead, or I will. And you will be safe, and the child, so that you can go home to Homana-Mujahr, to bear the child in safety and security. For Homana and the Cheysuli."

He kissed me, lay me down amidst the brush. Was gone.

Out of terrible pain I reached, snagged a sleeve, caught it, gripped it, dragged the arm it encased toward me, until it stiffened, and I could pull myself up a little.

"—Tynstar—" I gasped. "It was Tynstar—it was the Ihlini— "

I sagged, fell back, felt the texture of the velvet crusted with gems. And I knew.

In eight years, graying hair was grayer still, and beard. But the glittering eyes were the same. That, and the pride. The powerful arrogance that drives a man to madness all in the name of injured honor.

"It was Tynstar," I said. "Not you after all, my lord Mujhar . . . though the gods know you tried."

Beneath the beard and mustache, his lips were tight and flat. But they parted as he spoke. "I am glad," he said, "because now I know it was painful."

My own was suddenly bearable; the child was quiescent, as if it knew my father. Recognized the blood, the corrosiveness of the hatred, the virulence of the anger.

I took my hand from his sleeve, desiring not to touch him. Weakly, I asked. "What did he do to you . . . what did he do to you that was worth the extermination of a race . . . the destruction of a realm?" I drew in a difficult breath, willing the child to remain quiet. "Surely Ellic would have been satisfied with another bride . . . surely you are strong enough, resilient enough, to live your life without a liege man at your side . . . you are Mujhar, are you not? The Lion of Homana, save in human form . . ." Again, I sucked in air. "You have shapechanged your humility into arrogance, your humanity into obscenity . . ."

"Enough!" he cried. "Enough! What I did was for the good of Homana, for my realm . . . for the good of the Lion, so dishonored by a man, a shapechanger—" He broke it off, clearly walking the edge of the sword of sanity, and near to falling off. "Your suffering is deserved," he said plainly, "and I will relieve you of none of it."

"Once, I loved you," I told him. "More than I loved Hale, and the child I carry. But you have made that impossible. You have stripped me of everything you gave me, even that—"

"Enough!" he cried again. "You will bend your will to birthing that child, not wasting your strength on lies."

I nearly laughed at him; would have, had I the strength to do it. "You want this child so badly . . . a son for the Lion." Heavily, I swallowed, feeling pain washing in again, cramping breasts and belly. "But what if it is a girl? What if, after all these years, this pain, I give you a girl? Will you begin again, my lord? Will you use her for marriage bait, measuring the bidders one against the other, until you find the one you want? Like Ellic. Like Bellam—" I stopped, because if I tried to speak I would scream.

Hoarsely, he swore. "If this child is a girl I will give it to the beasts. The father was one—let the daughter know what it is!"

Hot tears ran down my temples, dampening hair already soaked with sweat. But I could not speak to deny him.

VI

He was already dead when I found him. And alone, so alone, lacking life, lacking *lir* . . . all he had now was the knowledge that he would never see the edge of madness, nor walk it, nor slip over to the other side, where Cheysuli as Homanans are stripped of dignity and humanity, becoming little more than brittle shells housing an absence of soul.

Once he had told me Cheysuli do not grieve, not as Homanans do, keening aloud for their loss. Cheysuli are an intensely private people, showing little of themselves except when it is necessary. For death, it was not; in private, they grieved, but rejoiced also, because the soul without a shell was now at home in the afterworld.

So I would not grieve aloud. But neither could I rejoice.

One of the women stirred. "My lord, the child is coming."

My father left the chamber.

VII

"Promise me," I begged. "Promise me you will see it to safety if the child is a girl."

Torrin's face was gray as he carried me through the corridor within my father's palace. Dampness trickled down my legs, staining the trews I wore.

"Promise me," I begged. "He will keep a boy—he *needs* a boy—but I fear for it if it is a girl . . . I swear, I think he is mad enough to kill it."

Still Torrin said nothing to me, speaking quietly to others, sending them all ahead.

"You *know* him," I said. "You know he will do it."

"No," he said at last. "The child is in no danger from Shaine. I swear, Lindir, that if he so much as *threatens* to harm the child, I will take it for my own."

I bit into my lip. "He will dismiss you."

His tone was very grim. "I will dismiss myself."

Tears ran down my face. "I want Hale," I whispered.

"So do I, Lindir. And so, I think, does Shaine, though he will never admit it. Not to kill, but to embrace; they were brothers in all but birth."

"Until I took him away."

"He took himself, and you. And no one, who had seen him with you, was surprised. Only Shaine. Only Shaine."

The pain was getting worse. "Is Lorsilla kind?"

"Aye, Lindir, she is kind. And I swear, she will help me. If the child is a girl, the Queen will help me take her."

"And if it is a boy?"

Torrin's voice was grimmer yet. "I will stay, if only to see that he is worthy of the Lion."

Through my pain, I smiled. "You sound like a Cheysuli."

"We are one and the same, I think. Shaped of

Homanan clay, fired by the gods. Shaine is a fool to think differently."

"Will we lose the war with Solinde? Bellam has Tynstar, now . . . Tynstar and the Ihlini."

His arms were tight around me. "I think we will lose the war."

It was almost a relief. "Well, if we do—" I broke off, sighing; so weary, now, of speech. So weary now of thinking. "Hale would say it will pave the way for the man who will win it back . . . and the man after him who will become the first Cheysuli Mujhar in nearly four hundred years."

Other voices swam nearer, saying things to Torrin. Things I did not know, drifting on tides of pain.

He put me down on the bed. Women were shooing him out. "You have my promise, lady. Now, it is time you bent your will to bringing forth a healthy child."

"For the Lion?"

"For us all."

He might have said something more, but the women had their way and chased him out of the chamber.

Leaving me to bear the child of prophecy: Hale's daughter, or his son.

I heard the infant's cry. Felt the blood gush out, hot, too quick, smelling sweet and thick. No one moved to staunch it.

"A girl," someone said. "Not a boy, a girl."

"Torrin!" I cried.

"The Mujhar will be angry."

"The Mujhar must be told."

Silence.

Then, "Who will tell the Mujhar?"

Too much blood . . . not so long now . . . "Torrin," I whispered. "Let it be Torrin who tells him."

The silence was disapproving.

I summoned up my strength. "Would you rather have it be me?"

The women knew better. So, I think, did I; the dead do not speak.

One of them held the girl, all sticky and smeared with blood. Sound of limb and lungs. The downy fuzz was dark; her eyes I could not see.

Not so long now . . . I stretched out a hand toward her. "I want—"

The Walker Behind

by Marion Zimmer Bradley

As one who on a lonesome road
Doth walk in fear and dread
And turns but once to look around
And turns no more his head
Because he knows a frightful fiend
Doth close behind him tread. . . .

Lythande heard the following footsteps that night on the road: a little pause so that if she chose, she could have believed it merely the echo of her own light footfall. Step-pause-step, and then, after a little hesitation, step-pause-step, step-pause-step.

And at first she did think it an echo, but when she stopped for a moment to assess the quality of the echo, it went on for at least three steps into the silence:

Step-pause-step; step-pause-step.

Not an echo, then, but someone, or some *thing*, following her. In the world of the Twin Suns, where encountering magic was rather more likely than not, magic was more often than not of the evil kind. In a lifetime spanning at least three ordinary lifetimes, Lythande had encountered a great deal of magic; she was by necessity a mercenary-magician, an Adept of the Blue Star, and by choice a minstrel; and she had discovered early in her life that good magic was the rarest of all encounters and seldom came her way. She had lived this long by developing very certain instincts; and her instincts told her that this footfall following her was not benevolent.

She had no notion of what it might be. The simplest solution was that someone in the last town she had passed through had developed a purely material grudge against her, and was following her on mischief bent, for some reason or no reason at all—perhaps a mere mortal distrust of magicians, or of magic, a condition not at all rare in Old Gandrin—and had chosen to take the law into his or her own hands and dispose of the unwelcome procurer of said magic. This was not at all rare, and Lythande had dealt with plenty of would-be assassins who wished to stop the magic by putting an effective stop to the magician; however powerful an Adept's magic, it could seldom survive a knife in the back. On the other hand, it could be handled with equal simplicity; after three ordinary lifetimes, Lythande's back had not yet become a sheath for knives.

So Lythande stepped off the road, loosening the first of her two knives in its scabbard—the simple white-handled knife, whose purpose was to handle purely material dangers of the road: footpads, assassins, thieves. She enveloped herself in the gray, cloudy folds of the hooded mage-robe, which made her look like a piece of the night itself, or a shadow, and stood waiting for the owner of the footsteps to come up with her.

But it was not that simple. Step-pause-step, and the footfalls died; the mysterious follower was pacing her. Lythande had hardly thought it would be so simple. She sheathed the white-handled knife again, and stood motionless, reaching out with all her specially trained senses to focus on the follower.

What she felt first was a faint electric tingle in the Blue Star that was between her brows; and a small, not quite painful crackle in her head. *The smell of magic*, she translated to herself; whatever was following, it was neither as simple, nor as easily disposed of, as an assassin with a knife.

She loosened the black-handled knife in the left-hand scabbard and, stepping herself like a ghost or a shadow, retraced her steps at the side of the road. This knife was especially fashioned for supernatural menaces, to kill ghosts and anything else from specters to were-wolves; no knife but this one could have taken her own life had she tired of it.

A shadow with an irregular step glided toward her, and Lythande raised the black-handled knife. It came plunging down, and the glimmer of the enchanted blade was lost in the shadow. There was a far-off, eerie cry that seemed to come, not from the shadow facing her on the dark road, but from some incredibly distant ghostly realm, to curdle the very blood in her veins, to wrench pain and lightnings from the Blue Star between her brows. Then, as that cry trembled into silence, Lythande felt the black handle of the knife come back into her hand, but a faint glimmer of moonlight showed her the handle alone: the blade had vanished, except for some stray drops of molten metal that fell slowly to the earth and vanished.

So the blade was gone, the black-handled knife that had slain unnumbered ghosts and other supernatural beings. Judging by the terrifying cry, Lythande had wounded her follower; but had she killed the thing that had eaten her magical blade? Anything that powerful would certainly be tenacious of life.

And if her black-handled knife would not kill it, it was unlikely it could be killed by any spell, protection, or magic she could command at the moment. It had been driven away, perhaps, but she could not be certain she had freed herself from it. No doubt, if she went on, it would continue to follow her, and one day it would catch up with her on some other lonesome road.

But for the moment she had exhausted her protection. And . . . Lythande glowered angrily at the black knife handle and the ruined blade . . . she had deprived herself needlessly of a protection that had never failed her before. Somehow she must manage to replace her enchanted knife before she again dared the roads of Old Gandrin by night.

For the moment—although she had traveled too far and for too long to fear anything she was *likely* to encounter on any ordinary night—she would be wiser to remove herself from the road. Such encounters as a mercenary-magician, particularly one such as Lythande, should expect were seldom of the likely kind.

So she went on in the darkness, listening for the hesitating step of the follower behind. There was only the vaguest and most distant sounds;

that blow, and that screech, indicated that while she had probably not destroyed her follower, she had driven it at least for a while into some other place. Whether it was dead, or had chosen to go and follow someone safer, for the moment Lythande neither knew nor cared.

The important thing at the moment was shelter. Lythande had been traveling these roads for many years, and remembered that many years ago there had been an inn somewhere hereabouts. She had never chosen, before this, to shelter there—unpleasant rumors circulated about travelers who spent the night at the inn and were never seen again, or seen in dreadfully altered form. Lythande had chosen to stay away; the rumors were none of her business, and Lythande had not survived this long in Old Gandrin without knowing the first rule of survival, which was to ignore everything but your *own* survival. On the rare occasions when curiosity or compassion had prompted her to involve herself in anyone else's fate, she had had all kinds of reason to regret it.

Perhaps her obscure destiny had guided her on this occasion to investigate these rumors. She looked down the black expanse of the road—without even moonlight—and saw a distant glimmer of light. Whether it was the inn of uncanny rumor, or whether it was the light of a hunter's campfire, or the lair of a were-dragon, there, Lythande resolved, she would seek shelter for the night. The last client to avail himself of her services as a mercenary-magician—a man who had paid her well to dehaunt his ancestral mansion—had left her with more than enough coin for a night at even the most luxurious inn; and if she could not pick up a commission to offset the cost of a night's shelter, she was no worse off. Besides, with the lute at her back, she could usually earn a supper and a bed as a minstrel; they were not common in this quarter.

A few minutes of brisk walking strengthened the vague light into a brilliantly shining lantern hung over a painted sign that portrayed the figure of an old woman driving a pig; the inn sign read the Hag and Swine. Lythande chuckled under her breath . . . the sign was comical enough, but it startled her that for such a cheerful sign there was no sound of music or jollity from inside; all was quiet as the very demon-haunted road itself. It made her remember again the very unsavory rumors about this very inn.

There was a very old story about a hag who indeed attempted to transform random travelers into swine, and other forms, but Lythande could not remember where she had heard that story. Well, if she, an Adept of the Blue Star, was no match for any roadside hag, whatever her propensity of increasing her herd of swine—or perhaps furnishing her table with pork—at the expense of travelers, she deserved whatever happened to her. Shouldering her lute and concealing the handle of the ruined knife in one of the copious pockets of the mage-robe, Lythande strode through the half-open door.

Inside, it was light, but only by contrast with the moonless darkness of the outdoors. The only light was firelight, from a hearth where a pale fire flickered with a dim and unpleasant flame. Gathered around the hearth were a collection of people, mere shapes in the dim room; but as Lythande's eyes adapted to the darkness, she began to make out forms, perhaps half a dozen men and women and a couple of shabby children; all had pinched faces, and pushed-in noses that were somehow porcine. From the dimness arose the tall, heavy form of a woman, clad in shapeless garments that seemed to hang on her anyhow, much patched and botched.

Ah, thought Lythande, *this innkeeper must be the hag. And those wretched children might very well be the swine.* Even secretly the jest pleased her.

In an unpleasant, snuffling voice, the tall hag demanded, "Who are you, sir, going about on the road where there be nowt but hants an' ghosts at this season?"

Lythande's first impulse was to gasp out, "I was *driven* here by evil magic; there is a monstrous Thing out there, prowling about this place!" But she managed to say instead, peacefully, "Neither hant nor ghost, but a wandering minstrel frightened like yourselves by the dangers of the road, and in need of supper and a night's lodging."

"At once, sir," said the hag, suddenly turning deferential. "Come to the fire and warm thyself."

Lythande came through the jostling crowd of small figures—yes, they were children, and at close range even more unpleasantly piglike; their sounds and snuffles made them even more animal. She felt a distinct revulsion for having them crowding against her. She was resigned to the "sir" with which the hag-innkeeper had greeted her; Lythande was the only woman ever to penetrate the mysteries of the Order of the Blue Star, and when (already sworn as an Adept, the Blue Star already blazing between her brows) she had been exposed as a woman, she was already protected against the worst they could have done. And so her punishment had been only this:

Be forever, then, had decreed the Master of the Star, *what you have chosen to seem; for on that day when any man save myself proclaims you a woman, then shall your magic be void and you may be slain and die.*

So for more than three ordinary lifetimes had Lythande wandered the roads as a mercenary-magician, doomed to eternal solitude; for she might reveal her true sex to no man, and while she might have a woman confidante if she could find one she could trust with her life, this exposed her chosen confidante to pressure from the many enemies of an Adept of the Blue Star; her first such confidante had been captured and tortured, and although she had died without revealing Lythande's secret, Lythande had been reluctant ever to expose another to that danger.

What had begun as a conscious masquerade was now her life; not a single gesture or motion revealed her as anything but the man she seemed —a tall, clean-shaven man with luxuriant fair hair, the blazing Blue Star between the high-arched shaven eyebrows, clad beneath the mage-robe in thigh-high boots, breeches, and a leather jerkin laced to reveal a figure muscular and broad-shouldered as an athlete, and apparently altogether masculine.

The innkeeper-hag brought a mug of drink and set it down before Lythande. It smelled savory and steamed hot; evidently a mulled wine with spices, a specialty of the house. Lythande lifted it to her lips, only pretending to sip; one of the many vows fencing about the powers of an Adept of the Blue Star was that they might never be seen to eat or drink in the presence of any man. The drink smelled good—as did the food she could smell cooking somewhere—and Lythande resented, not for the first time, the law that often condemned her to long periods of thirst and hunger; but she was long accustomed to it and recalling the singular name and reputation of this establishment, and the old story about the hag and swine, perhaps it was just as well to shun such food or drink as might be found in this place; it was by their greed, if she remembered the tale rightly, that the travelers had found themselves transformed into pigs.

The greedy snuffling of the hoglike children, if that was what they were, served as a reminder, and listening to it, she felt neither thirsty nor hungry. It was her custom at such inns to order a meal served in the privacy of her chamber, but she decided that in this place she would not indulge it; in the pockets of her mage-robe she kept a small store of dried fruit and bread, and long habit had accustomed her to snatching a hurried bite whenever she could do so unobserved.

She took a seat at one of the rough tables near the fireplace, the pot of ale before her, and, now and again pretending to take a sip of it, asked, "What news, friends?"

Her encounter fresh in her mind, she half expected to be told of some monster haunting the roadway. But nothing was volunteered. Instead, a rough-looking man seated on the opposite bench from hers, on the other side of the fireplace, raised his pot of ale and said, "Your health, sir; it's a bad night to be out. Storm coming on, unless I'm mistaken. And I've been traveling these roads, man and boy, for forty years."

"Oh?" inquired Lythande courteously. "I am new to these parts. Are the roads generally safe?"

"Safe enough," he grunted, "unless the folks get the idea you're a jewel carrier or some such." He needed to add no more; there were always thieves who might take the notion that some person was not so poor as he sought to appear (so as to seem to have nothing worth stealing), and cut him open looking for his jewels.

"And you?"

"I travel the roads as my old father did; I am a dog barber." He spoke the words truculently. "Anyone who has a dog to show or to sell knows I can make the beast look to its best advantage." Someone behind his back snickered, and he drew himself up to his full height and proclaimed, "It's a respectable profession."

"One of your kind," said a man before the fire, "sold my old father an old dog with rickets and the mange, for a healthy watchdog: the old critter hardly had the strength to bark."

"I don't sell dogs," said the man haughtily. "I only prepare them for show—"

"And o'course you'd never stoop to faking a mongrel up to look like a purebred, or fixing up an old dog with the mange to look like a young one with glossy topknots and long hair," said the heckler ironically. "Everybody in this country knows that when you have some bad old stock to get rid of, stolen horses to paint with false marks, there's old Gimlet the dog faker, worse than any gypsy for tricks—"

"Hey there, don't go insulting honest gypsies with your comparisons," said a dark man seated on a box on the floor by the fire and industriously eating a rich-smelling stew from a wooden bowl; he had a gold earring in his ear like one of that maligned race. "We trade horses all up and down this country from here to Northwander, and I defy any man to say he ever got a bad horse from any of our tribe."

"Gimlet the dog barber, are ye?" asked another of the locals, a shabby, squint-eyed man. "I've been looking for you; don't you remember me?"

The dog barber put on a defiant face. "Afraid not, friend."

"I had a bitch last year had thirteen pups," said the newcomer, scowling. "Good bitch; been the pride and joy of my family since she was a pup. You said you'd fix her up a brew so she'd get her milk in and be able to feed them all—"

"Every dog handler learns something of the veterinary art," said Gimlet. "I can bring in a cow's milk, too, and—"

"Oh, I make no doubt you can shoe a goose, too, to hear you tell it," the man said.

"What's your complaint, friend? Wasn't she able to feed her litter?"

"Oh, aye, she was," said the complainer. "And for a couple of days, it felt good watching every little pup sucking away at her tits; then it occurred to me to count 'em, and there were no more than eight pups."

Gimlet restrained a smile.

"I said only that I would arrange matters so the bitch could feel all her brood; if I disposed of the runts who would have been unprofitable, without you having to harrow yourself by drowning them—" Gimlet began.

"Don't you go weaseling out of it," the man said, clenching his fists. "Any way you slice it, you owe me for at least five good pups."

Gimlet looked round. "Well, that's as may be" he said. "Maybe tomorrow we can arrange something. It never occurred to me you'd get chesty about the runts in the litter, more than any bitch could raise. Not unless you've a childless wife or young daughter who wants to cosset something and hankers to feed 'em with an eye-dropper and dress 'em in doll's clothes; more trouble than it's worth, most folks say. But here's my hand on it." He stuck out his hand with such a friendly, open smile of good faith that Lythande was enormously entertained; between the rogue and the yokel, Lythande, after years spent traveling the roads, was invariably on the side of the rogue. The disgruntled dog owner hesitated a moment, but finally shook his hand and called for another pot of beer for all the company.

Meanwhile the hag-innkeeper, hovering to see if it would come to some kind of fight, and looking just a little disappointed that it had not, stopped at Lythande's side.

"You, sir, will be wanting a room for the night?"

Lythande considered. She did not particularly like the look of the place, and if she spent the night, resolved she would not feel safe in closing her eyes. On the other hand, the dark road outside was less attractive than ever, now that she had tasted the warmth of the fireside. Furthermore, she had lost her magical knife, and would be unprotected on the dark road with some *thing* following.

"Yes," she said, "I will have a room for the night."

The price was arranged—neither cheap nor outrageous—and the innkeeper asked, "Can I find you a woman for the night?"

This was always the troublesome part of traveling in male disguise. Lythande, whatever her romantic desires, had no wish for the kind of women kept in country inns for traveling customers, without choice; they were usually sold into this business as soon as their breasts grew, if not before. Yet it was a singularity to refuse this kind of accommodation, and one that could endanger the long masquerade on which her power depended.

Tonight she did not feel like elaborate excuses.

"No, thank you; I am weary from the road and will sleep." She dug into her robe for a couple of spare coins. "Give the girl this for her trouble."

The hag bowed. "As you will, sir, Frennet! Show the gentleman to the south room."

A handsome girl, tall and straight and slender, with silky hair looped up into elaborate curls, rose from the fireside and gestured with a shapely arm half concealed by silken draperies. "This way, if ye please," she said, and Lythande rose, edging between Gimlet and the dog owner. In a pleasant, mellow voice, she wished the company good night.

The stairs were old and rickety, stretching up several flights, but had once been stately—about four owners ago, Lythande calculated. Now they were hung with cobwebs, and the higher flights looked as if they might be the haunt of bats, too.

From one of the posts at a corner landing, a dark form ascended, flapping its wings, and cried out in a hoarse, croaking sound:

"*Good evening, ladies! Good evening, ladies!*"

The girl Frennet raised an arm to warn off the bird.

"That accursed jackdaw! Madame's pet, sir; pay no attention," she said good-naturedly, and Lythande was glad of the darkness. It was beneath the dignity of an Adept of the Blue Star to take notice of a trained bird, however articulate.

"Is that all it says?"

"Oh no, sir; quite a vocabulary the creature has, but then, you see, you never know what it's going to say, and sometimes it can really startle you if you ain't expecting it," said Frennet, opening the door to a large, dark chamber. She went inside and lighted a candelabrum standing by the huge, draped four-poster. The jackdaw flapped in the doorway and croaked hoarsely, "*Don't go in there, Madame! Don't go in there, Madame!*"

"Just let me get rid of her for you, sir," said Frennet, taking up a broom and making several passes with it, attempting to drive the jackdaw back down the staircase. Then she noticed that Lythande was still standing in the doorway of the room.

"It's all right, sir; you can go right in. You don't want to let her scare you. She's just a stupid bird."

Lythande had stopped cold, however, not so much because of the bird as because of the sharp prickling of the Blue Star between her brows. *The smell of magic*, she thought, wishing she were a hundred leagues from the Hag and Swine; without her magical knife, she was unwilling to spend a minute, let alone a night, in a room that smelled evilly of magic as that one did.

She said pleasantly, "I am averse to the omens, child. Could you perhaps show me to another chamber where I might sleep? After all, the inn is far from full, so find me another room, there's a good girl."

"Well, I dunno what the mistress would say," began Frennet dubiously, while the bird shrieked, *"There's a good girl! There's a clever girl!"* Then she smiled and said, "But what she dunna know won't hurt her, I reckon. This way."

Up another flight of stairs, and Lythande felt the numbing prickling of the Blue Star, *the smell of magic,* recede and drop away. The rooms on this floor were lighted and smaller, and Frennet turned into one of them.

"Me own room, sir; yer welcome to the half of my bed if you wish it, an' no obligation. I mean—I heard ye say ye didn't want a woman, but you sent a tip for me, and—" She stopped, swallowed, and said determinedly, her face flushing, "I dunno why yer traveling like a man, ma'am. But I reckon ye have yer reasons, an' they's none of my business. But ye came here in good faith for a night's lodgin', and I think ye've a right to that and nothing else." The girl's face was red and embarrassed. "I swore no oath to keep my mouth shut about what's goin' on here, and I don't want your death on my hands, so there."

"My death?" Lythande said. "What do you mean, child?"

"Well, I'm in for it now," Frennet said, "but ye've

a right to know, ma'am—sir—noble stranger. Folk who sleep here don't come back no more human; did ye see those little children down yonder? They're only halfway changed; the potions don't work all that well on children. I saw you didn't drink yer wine; so when they came to drive you out to the sty, you'd still be human and they'd kill you—or drive you out in the dark, where the Walker Behind can have ye."

Shivering, Lythande recalled the entity that had destroyed her magical knife. That, then, had been the Walker Behind.

"What is this—this Walker Behind?" she asked.

"I dunno, ma'am. Only it *follows*, and draws folk into the other world, thass all I know. Ain't nobody ever come back to tell what it is. Only I hears 'em scream when it starts followin' them."

Lythande stared about the small, mean chamber. Then she asked, "How did you know that I was a woman?"

"I dunno, ma'am. I always knows, that's all. I always know, no matter what. I won't tell the missus; I promise."

Lythande sighed. Perhaps the girl was somewhat psychic; she had accepted a long time ago that while her disguise was usually opaque to men, there would always be a few women who for one reason or another would see through it. Well, there was nothing to be done about it, unless she were willing to murder the girl, which she was not.

"See that do you not; my life depends on it," she said. "But perhaps you need not give up your bed to me either; can you guide me unseen out of this place?"

"That I can, ma'am, but it's a wretched night to be out, and the Walker Behind in the dark out there. I'd hate to hear you screamin' when it comes to take you away."

Lythande chuckled, but mirthlessly. "Perhaps instead you would hear *it* screaming when I came to take *it*," she said. "I think that is what I encountered before I came here."

"Yes'm. It drives folk in here because it wants 'em, and then it takes their souls. I mean, when they're turned into pigs, I guess they don't need their souls no more, see? And the Walker Behind takes them."

"Well, it will not take me," Lythande said briefly. "Nor you, if I can manage it. I encountered this thing before I came here; it took my knife, so I must somehow get another."

"They's plenty of knives in the kitchen, ma'am," Frennet said. "I can take ye out through there."

Together they stole down the stairs, Lythande moving like a ghost in the silence that had caused many people to swear that they had seen Lythande seem to disappear into thin air. In the parlor most of the guests had gone to rest; she heard a strange grunting sound. Upstairs there were curious grunting noises; on the morrow, Lythande supposed, they would be driven out to the sty, their souls left for the Walker Behind and their bodies to reappear as sausages or roast pork. In the kitchen, as they passed it, Lythande saw the innkeeper—the hag. She was chopping herbs; the pungent scent made Lythande think of the pungent drink she had fortunately not tasted.

So why had this evil come to infest this country? Her extended magical senses could now hear the step in the dark, prowling outside: the Walker Behind. She could sense and feel its evil circling in the dark, awaiting its monstrous feast of souls. But how—and why?—had anything human, even that hag, come to join hands with such a ghastly thing of damnation?

There had been a saying in the Temple of the Star that there was no fathoming the depths either of Law or of Chaos. And surely the Walker Behind was a thing from the very depths of Chaos; and Lythande, as a Pilgrim Adept, was solemnly sworn to uphold forever and defend Law against Chaos even at the Final Battle at the end of the world.

"There are some things," she observed to the girl Frennet, "that I would prefer not to encounter until the Final Battle where Law will defeat Chaos at world's end. And of those things the Walker Behind is first among them; but the ways of Chaos do not await my convenience; and if I encounter it now, at least I need not meet it at the end of the world." She stepped quietly into the kitchen, and the hag jerked up her head.

"You? I thought you was sleeping by now, magician. I even sent you the girl—"

"Don't blame the girl; she did as you bade her," Lythande said. "I came hither to the Hag and Swine, though I knew it not, to rid the world of a pigsty of Chaos. Now you shall feed your own evil servant."

She gestured, muttering the words of a spell; the hag flopped forward on all fours, grunting and snuffling. Outside in the dark, Lythande sensed the approach of the great evil Thing, and motioned to Frennet.

"Open the door, child."

Frennet flung the door open; Lythande shoved the grunting thing outside over the threshold. There was a despairing scream—half animal but dreadfully half human—from somewhere; then only the body of a pig remained grunting in the foggy darkness of the innyard. From the shadowy Walker outside, there was a satisfied croon that made Lythande shudder. Well, so much for the Hag and Swine; she had deserved it.

"There's nothing left of her, ma'am."

"She deserves to be served up as sausages for breakfast, dressed with her own herbs," Lythande remarked, looking at what was left, and Frennet shook her head.

"I'd have no stomach for her meself, ma'am."

The jackdaw flapped out into the kitchen crying, *"Clever girl! Clever girl! There's a good girl!"* and Lythande said, "I think if I had my way, I'd wring that bird's neck. There's still the Walker to deal with; she was surely not enough to satisfy the appetite of—that thing."

"Maybe not, ma'am," Frennet said, "but you could deal with her; can you deal with it? It'll want your soul more than hers, mighty magician as you must be."

Lythande felt serious qualms; the innkeeper-hag, after all, had been but a small evil. But in her day, Lythande had dealt with a few large evils, though seldom any as great and terrifying as the Walker. And this one had already taken her magical knife. Had the spells weakened it any?

A long row of knives was hanging on the wall; Frennet took down the longest and most formidable, proffering it to her, but Lythande shook her head, passing her hand carefully along the row of knives. Most knives were forged for material uses only, and she did not think any of them would be much use against this great magic out of Chaos.

The Blue Star between her brows tingled, and she stopped, trying to identify the source of the magical warning. Was it only that she could hear, out in the darkness of the innyard, the characteristic step of the Walker Behind?

Step-pause-step.

Step-pause-step.

No, the source was closer than that. It lay—moving her head cautiously, Lythande identified the source—the cutting board that lay on the table; the hag had been cutting her magical herbs, the one to transform the unwary into swine. Slowly, Lythande took up the knife; a common kitchen one with a long, sharp blade. All along the blade was the greenish mark of the herb juices. From the pocket of her mage-robe, Lythande took the ruined handle—the elaborately carved hilt with magical runes—of her ruined knife, looked at it with a sigh—she had always been proud of the elegance of her magical equipment, and this was hearth-witch, or kitchen-magic at best—and flung it down with the kitchen remnants.

Frennet clutched at her. "Oh, don't go out there, ma'am! It's still out there a-waiting for you."

And the jackdaw, fluttering near the hearth, shrieked, *Don't go out there! Oh, don't go out there!*"

Gently, Lythande disengaged the girl's arms. "You stay here," she said. "You have no magical protection; and I can give you none." She drew the mage-robe's hood closely about her head, and stepped into the foggy innyard.

It was there, she could feel it waiting, circling, prowling, its hunger a vast evil maw to be filled. She knew it hungered for her, to take in her body, her soul, her magic. If she spoke, she might find herself in its power. The knife firmly gripped in her hand, she traced out a pattern of circling steps, sunwise in spite of the darkness. If she could hold the Thing of darkness in combat till sunrise, the very light might destroy it; but it could not be much after midnight. She had no wish to hold this dreadful Thing at bay till sunrise, even if her powers should prove equal to it.

So it must be dispatched at once . . . and she hoped, since she had lost her own magical knife, with the knife she had taken from the monstrous Thing's own accomplice. Alone in the fog, despite the bulky warmth of the mage-robe, Lythande felt her body dripping with ice—or was it only terror? Her knees wobbled, and the icy drips seemed to course down between her shoulders, which spasmed as if expecting a knife driven between them. Frennet, shivering in the light of the doorway, was watching her with a smile, as if she had not the slightest doubt.

Is this what men feel when their women are watching them? Certainly, if she should call the Thing to her and fail to destroy it, it would turn next on the girl, and for all she knew, on the jackdaw, too; and neither of them deserved death, far less soul-destruction. The girl was innocent, and the jackdaw only a dumb creature . . . well, a harmless creature; dumb it wasn't; it was still crying out gibberish.

"Oh, my soul, it's coming! It's coming! Don't go out there!"

It was coming; the Blue Star between her brows was prickling like live coals, the blue light burning through her brain from the inside out. Why, in the name of all the gods that ever were or weren't, had she ever thought she wanted to be a magician? Well, it was years too late to ask that. She clenched her hand on the rough wooden handle of the kitchen knife of the kitchen hag, and thrust up roughly into the greater darkness that was the Walker, looming over her and shadowing the whole of the innyard.

She was not sure whether the great scream that enveloped the world was her own scream of terror, or whether it came from the vast dark vortex that whirled around the Walker; she was enveloped in a monstrous whirlwind that swept her *off* her feet and into dark fog and dampness. She had time for a ghostly moment of dread—suppose the herbs on the blade should transform the Walker into a great Hog of Chaos? And how could she meet it if it did? But this was the blade of the Walker's own accomplice in his own magic of Chaos; she thrust into the Thing's heart and, buffeted and battered by the whirlwinds of Chaos, grimly hung on.

Then there was a sighing sound, and something unreeled and was gone. She was standing in the innyard, and Frennet's arms were hugging hard.

The jackdaw shrieked, *It's gone! It's gone! Oh, good girl, good girl!*

It was gone. The innyard was empty of magic, only fog on the moldering stones. There was a shadow in the kitchen behind Frennet; Lythande went inside and saw, wrapped in his cloak and ready to depart, the pudgy face and form of Gimlet, the dog faker.

"I was looking for the innkeeper," he said truculently. "This place is too noisy for me; too much going on in the halls; and there's the girl. You," he said crossly to Frennet. "Where's your mistress? And I thought you were to join me."

Frennet said sturdily, "I'm me own mistress now, sir. And I ain't for sale, not any more. As for the mistress, I dunno where she is; you can go and ask for her at the gates of Heaven, an' if you don't find her there—well, you know where you can go."

It took a minute for that to penetrate his dull understanding; but when it did, he advanced on her with a clenched fist.

"Then I been robbed of your price!"

Lythande reached into the pockets of the magerobe. She handed him a coin.

"Here, you've made a profit on the deal, no doubt—as you always do. Frennet is coming with me."

Gimlet stared and finally pocketed the coin, which—Lythande could tell from his astonished eyes—was the biggest he had ever seen.

"Well, good sir, if you say so. I got to be off about my dogs. I wonder if I could get some breakfast first."

Lythande gestured to the joints of meat hanging along the wall of the kitchen. "There's plenty of ham, at least."

He looked up, gulped and shuddered. "No thanks." He slouched out into the darkness, and Lythande gestured to the girl.

"Let's be on our way."

"Can I really come with you?"

"For a while, at least," Lythande said. The girl deserved that. "Go quickly, and fetch anything you want to take."

"Nothing from here," she said. "But the other customers—"

"They'll turn human again now that the hag's dead, such of 'em as haven't been served up for roast pork," Lythande said. "Look there." And indeed, the joints of ham hanging along the wall had taken on a horrible and familiar look, not porcine at all. "Let's get out of here."

They strode down the road toward the rising sun, side by side, the jackdaw fluttering after, crying out, *"Good morning, ladies! Good morning, ladies."*

"Before the sun rises," Lythande said. "I shall wring that bird's neck."

"Oh, aye," Frennet said. "Or dumb it wi' your magic. May I ask why you travel in men's clothes, Lady?"

Lythande smiled and shrugged.

"Wouldn't you?"

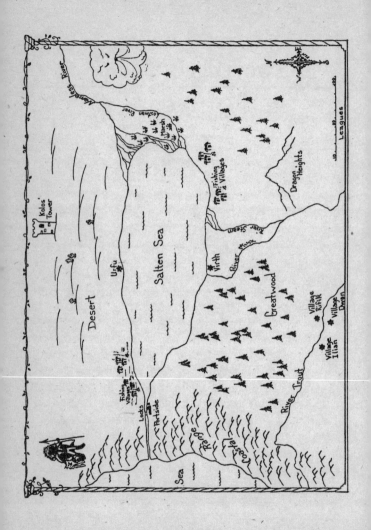

Two-edged Choice

By Ru Emerson

Prince Ilforic's Dispensers of Justice and Collectors of Tax had been gone for four or five days. Long enough that Liatt should have been able to take that deep breath Jahno had taken once he'd seen them out of sight. Long enough she could put them out of her mind. Even the ordinary villagers had begun to find other topics for gossip. Liatt was worried.

But it wasn't the little huddle of velvet-clad nobles and their attendant soldiery that had worried her. Unlike Jahno, Liatt knew the Prince wasn't interested in one aging sergeant who had finally taken the permanent leave someone forgot to give him—not after ten years. No, if Ilforic had been out to make an example of Jahno he would never have waited so long to look for him. There had been a small detachment to soldiers, two seasons after they'd come back to Jahno's old village, and they had asked plenty of questions. They hadn't really looked too hard, and there hadn't been any since.

No. Liatt hadn't started to worry until the Dispensers and so on were on their way to the next set of villages, seven leagues through the southern corner of Greatwood and halfway to the coast. *Poor fragile flowers, their noses must be starting to unwrinkle by now,* she thought wryly. Amazing how sensitive noble noses seemed to be. The pigs old Dame Husa kept behind her small tavern in Village Ilian had been enough to send them scurrying to smaller Rifik, to seek lodging in the second best inn in the area. Well, that might keep Jahno's younger brother quiet a while about coin and his lack of it. Madda—no. Nothing would *ever* keep Jahno's harpy of a mother silent for long.

Liatt went about her morning chores automatically; her mind was still on that delegation and the odd things that had happened after it left.

Of course, it was odd in the first place that a Prince's Delegation should come here; that hadn't happened in over five years. Perhaps Ilforic was tightening his grip on his little kingdom, perhaps that was all. Like they'd said. All the same, she'd been glad to avoid them, fearing anyone who might recognize the family features under so many years of fighting and farming; she'd kept prudently in the background when it was impossible to avoid the Delegation, otherwise stayed home, claiming her best breeding cow as cause.

She ran practiced hands over its buff-colored hide, her mind less than half on the beast. Still not dropping; no reason she should have had so much difficulty. Liatt had already promised out the calf for a good price, and she needed that coin, all the moreso since her best bitch had died over the winter. She'd have to replace the dog, soon; the cow was her last source of easy silver between now and winter.

Well, it *was* odd. There hadn't been two matters to work up for a Delegate Court, and the nobles conducting it—according to her sister-in-law—had looked and probably been hellishly bored. The taxes always went to Dame Hulse's inn, twice a year, and were sent on by the Prince's messenger on his monthly pass-by at the end of the next month. There was no need to send a Delegation to make certain of the taxes.

She might be taking alarm for no cause. Jahno certainly told her so, whenever he thought of it. All very well for him; his single act of leaving his company without consent was nothing compared to some of the things she'd done over a long and checkered career.

And since Ilforic's men had left—dreams, strange and ugly dreams, and a sense of being watched down in the woods near the creek. The bird that came down the chimney and sat stunned on the hearth until Jahno scooped it up and threw it out; he claimed not to have seen the malevolent gleam in its eye, and perhaps he hadn't. Poor innocent wouldn't have expected it; she did, and he accused her of too much ale with her stew.

The Delegation itself couldn't have been looking for a woman of forty years, a woman of hard aspect, harder visage and blade-strengthened hands. Someone traveling with it was, she was becoming increasingly certain of that. But why, and for whom?

Middle years, small, dark, strong hands—that might be any middle-aged village woman. Add sword scars, knife cuts—the odds of finding would narrow considerably. Liatt scowled at the hands rubbing the cow's flank: A long, white scar—jagged and nearly a finger's tip at its widest—ran across the back of her left hand and up past her wrist. Another—less visible, particularly when she'd been in the barn for an hour or so—cut straight across the backs of all four fingers, right hand. Old scars—*before I learned how to fight properly*—but as distinctive as mismatched eyes. Or red hair, or blonde, in this end of the world. At least she didn't have that distinction; hers was as black and thick as any native-born woman's—as black as Jahno's. Her eyes were darker, brown to Jahno's dark blue, but that was nothing to mark her out at a distance. Village women did not look Delegation nobles in the eye.

A small noise brought her around in a half crouch, her right hand still on the cow, left reaching for the dagger she'd put at her belt. It took a moment to find the source: a bird had got itself inside the barn, and was trying to batter its way up through the welter of braces and cross-braces to the hole in the roof. As she watched, it made it; it was staggering as it walked around the edge of the break in the thatching. For several moments it sat still on the edge of the hole. Liatt dropped her dagger back into its sheath and walked outside, shading her eyes against the early sun, watched as it flew off. It circled the house three times, high up, and soared off across the edge of the woods.

It looked like an ordinary sparrow. But it had circled three times, and she'd felt a strong backwash of power.

She stepped back to lean against the barn and chewed at her lower lip. Suddenly, it all fell into place. "That was sent by a wizard, I know the smell of it. Ah, hells, Kolos! Is it you again?" No answer, save her breathing and the cow shifting uncomfortably in its stall. She walked away from the barn, stalked into the small house she and Jahno shared, for the first time in ten long years ignoring the needs of her animals. There was something at the moment more important than a cow, even that particular cow. Daggers.

She cursed, fluently and imaginatively, all the way from barn door to house door, all the way up the narrow stair that led to her personal storage cubby behind the strings of dried meat and vegetables, behind the baskets of wrinkled apples. Cursed as she dragged the small chest out of its niche and flung the lid back. Was still mumbling as she found the fat rawhide packet and undid its tie. "Nasty dreams, and Jahno says it's an overly spiced joint, or too much ale! Hah! Funny little things out in the barn, and he tries to tell me my *eyes* are going, as though I were getting *old!*" She was half cursing Jahno right along with Kolos as she started sorting through the welter of blades, sheaths, and straps.

What clothing she wore these days wasn't as well suited to the hiding and quick release of half her store. It would have to do. She needed the practice, but her old fighting leathers would cause comment all the way to the Salten Sea, if anyone happened to see her. And doubtless, they would. "Bloody narrow-minded peasants! Bloody narrow-minded peasant of a husband! Bloody, rotten Kolos, you waited on purpose! Couldn't take me at thirty, so you waited ten years, may your latest boy weary of you and put rash-oak in your bath oil!" Two knives vanished up her left sleeve, another two up the right. She mumbled over the next ones, finally sorted them out enough to add another to her left boot, attach one to the inside of her right, two to the outside. Another to the inside of her left thigh. One—it was still uncomfortable, wearing one there—just inside the collar, at the back of her neck. The baldric that went inside a shirt and held four more she would have to leave for now; the shirt she wore absolutely would not open low enough, and there wasn't enough room in it for the daggers and her, too.

She stood, examined herself critically and swore again. "This is ridiculous. I've gained breast; probably cut one off trying to get a dagger out of my shirt, damn you, Kolos, may your next spell backfire on you!"

She sighed heavily, clomped down the stairs and back outdoors. Jahno was across the village, helping dear Madda with her wretched sheep shearing—something Liatt absolutely refused to deal with. *Bugs in the fleeces; ticks and things. Ugh!* For once, it didn't bother her that Jahno still hopped to Madda's bidding as if he were ten years old; today she didn't want him around. She glanced around, strode back through the barn, and out into the woods behind it.

Two hours later, she was still mumbling curses under her breath, but less often: it took air she didn't have. Her hands and arms hurt. Ten years of living in a small village, caring for her cows and dogs, mucking out, planting and weeding the garden patch, splitting the firewood Jahno felled—it had kept her strong, but it hadn't kept the right muscles in shape. She finally pulled knives out of the slender aspen she'd been using for a target—and the four out of the muddy ground that had missed entirely—and shagged her boots off so she could go stand in the stream.

It helped, immediately; she stooped to bring up two cupped handfuls and splash her face, emptied another double handful over the back of her head. "Well." She let the air out in a rush, dug both hands into the back of her waist to knead the muscles there. "Not totally out of shape, are you? Not good, though! One of those slimy little boys Kolos used to hire could gut you easy, just now." Not a very reassuring thought, that: Kolos would no doubt still be hiring that kind of nasty-minded pretty boy to wield sword for him, but unless his fortune'd gone down, he'd be able to afford *good* ones now.

But if she pushed it any more today, she'd be too stiff tomorrow to use her hands—that wasn't sense. And she wasn't getting any looser this afternoon, she'd passed that point an hour back. With a weary sigh, she scooped more water over the back of her neck, yelped as it ran down her back, and waded ashore. Boots—carry them back, she never had cared for wet feet inside her boots.

She pushed back through the thick brush that lined the stream banks and stopped to wipe the mud from her feet when the least of noises brought her around again: this time, she had a thin-bladed dagger in each hand, and had come down into the tight fighting stance.

Jahno blinked at her, took an involuntary step backward and nearly fell. Liatt sheathed one of the blades and caught his arm. She was laughing as she steadied him. "Little green gods, I'm not so slow at that, am I?"

"Guh—*gods*, Li, what are you doing out here?" Jahno pulled free of her grasp. He'd gone white when she turned on him and was still rather pale. "I didn't find you at the barn, and I thought maybe you'd come down to bathe, and—*gods*, Li! If anyone saw you like that!"

"If they did, they'd be trespassing, wouldn't they? Seems to me I made it clear years ago this is our little stretch of water, and I don't want to wash with half the village watching." She slid the other knife home, brushed wet hair off her brow. Her nose crinkled. "Speaking of water and bathing, you reek of sheep, Jahno."

He didn't look pleased himself. "I know it. Got to wash down, and you'll have to go over my back for ticks later—sorry, Li."

"What was wrong with the boys? Oh, never mind! I'll do it." She hated de-ticking Jahno, going over him a bit of clear, pale skin at a time, a smoking hot bit of stick in her hand to touch them with to make them pull out. Hated it. But even when his nephews traded him the onerous task, she still had to check. The innkeeper's sons were too young to take ticks seriously. Liatt and the village healer had nursed Jahno through one attack of tick fever, once was definitely enough. On top of nursing Jahno, she'd had her chores, his—the trade wasn't an even one, and his nephews seldom came out to aid Jahno's household.

Of course, they weren't supposed to be kin. Jahno probably had been a hunted man, those first few years. That was why his younger brother

Eghen had the inn in Jahno's rightful place, and why Jahno felled firewood and worked for the village smith.

Ticks, she thought tiredly. "Well? What's wrong with you?" Jahno was still standing, staring at her as though he'd never seen her before.

"I asked, you didn't say, Li. Those," he gestured nervously toward her right sleeve, where the daggers hid. "You haven't had them out in ten years, Li. Why now?"

"Later. Not out here, all right? Besides—you don't know I haven't had them out in ten years. Just not around you." Her feet were dry and reasonably clean; she sat on the log he'd tripped over, pulled the boots on. The left one still was hard to work on, the inside knife sheath never *had* fit right. *Damn.* She was limping slightly because of it. "I'll get a couple sticks hot, get you some real bathing water in the copper."

"I don't need—"

"If you want to sleep on the floor tonight, you don't need hot water and soap. If you plan to sleep with me, though—I told you, once, didn't I?"

"You told me," he admitted with a sigh. "No sheep. Sorry, Li. Frankly, I don't like the smell much myself, never did. I'm just tired, and it sounds more work than it's worth. All I want is something to eat and bed."

"You'll feel better sleeping clean. Madda didn't feed you?" She tried to keep the irritation out of her voice. By Jahno's expression, she hadn't done a very good job of it. He made a wry face, shrugged.

"Something, hours ago. What Madda considers food. I thought of stopping at the inn, but I felt too grubby and Eghen's last batch of ale's a little sour. Don't know why he can't stick to Father's way of making it."

"Yours is better anyway. I'll draw you a pot. There's a fresh loaf, the cooper's wife traded me for eggs." She gave him a shove, not unfriendly, and a brief smile. "Go wash, the cold water feels great. I'll see you up at the house. Did you check on the cow?" He shook his head. "Kedru come back with you?" He rolled his eyes. "Well?"

"He did that much."

She sighed. He had liked most of her dogs; for some reason, this last of poor dead Michat's litter annoyed him to no end. "Was he out of line today?" He shook his head. "He's young; he'll train." Jahno just flipped a hand at her, shook his head again in disbelief and pushed through the brush. She heard him squawk as cold water hit him.

It was cool in the woods, even in the rare places the sun came through; she looked up before stepping into the clearings, but even though she felt watched, she saw no one, and the bird—well, if it was up there, she couldn't see it. *What are you, scared?* she snarled at herself. She curled her hands, gingerly, opened them both flat, and pressed the palms together, stretched them. Sore already; not good.

The cow was shifting, so was her burden. Tonight, late, or early in the morning. Liatt gave her a pat on her way through.

Just into the yard between shed and house, a hairy, dark bundle came hurtling across the open, threw itself at her, yelping joyously. Liatt got a knee up between them, caught at the thick ruff with both hands and dropped to her knees, pulling the dog down with her. "Way I taught you, hmmm? Taught you to jump on me like that? *No jump!*" The dog let its ears flag, but only briefly; a long red tongue caught the side of her face. She swatted at it halfheartedly. "None of that, either! Dog spit all over me!" Kedru wriggled and lunged for her again, but missed as her grip tightened on his ruff and dragged him back. "Guard dog, hah. Haven't got the brains, have you?" Kedru wriggled again, an incredibly stupid dog-smile splitting his face. His tongue lolled. "Come on, we'll get Jahno a bath, eh?" And, as the dog pulled the one word out he could understand, and hung back, she laughed. "Not for you, stupid! For Jahno!" That was confusing, no words there a young dog could follow, but the tone of voice was encouraging. Kedru scrambled after Liatt, bouncing back a few paces after she cuffed him for catching her heels and nearly tripping her.

Brainless pup. He had Michat's dark brown and black coloring, her cheerful smile that made her kind so popular—but none of Michat's intelligence, at least not yet. That had been the real selling point for Michat's pups: they guarded households in need, or children sent berrying, or herds. One of Michat's earlier pups helped the blind old minstrel Jessamyn around, and sat quietly at his feet while he sang for weddings and feasts. Kedru—well, all right, he wasn't the smartest of Michat's pups, and he *was* young. She needed time with him, and lately there hadn't been any.

She got the copper filled from the yard tank, got

the fire blown back up from its bed of ash and clinkers, split some more dry wood for it. The loaf could go on the settle, so they'd have it warm; what was left of the joint would be fine cold. Like as not Madda had fed the men those awful little pasties of hers. Stupid woman had delusions of gentility, the pasties were small even for a lady's appetite, and no one could ever convince her that the quality of meat mattered, if it was cut small and buried in gravy. Liatt firmly believed Madda'd killed off Jahno's father by feeding him a ripe mutton pasty.

She ordered Kedru out—to her surprise, he went the first time—and shut the lower door on him. She didn't quite trust him yet around a joint, he'd taken one off the settle the month before. The water was steaming, the bread making a pleasant smell by the time Jahno came back in, bootless, hatless and shirtless, his hair soaked.

"You still haven't answered me," he said. Liatt had the lantern lit, despite the early hour, so she could make certain she had the last of the ticks. Jahno, still damp from his bath, was all goose bumps as the evening wind slid over bare skin.

"Answered?"

"Come on, Li. Knives. Daggers. What were you doing out there?"

"Practicing. Something's wrong." He started to turn; she grabbed his arm, turned him back. "Hold still, I'm almost finished."

"Hope so." It was taking effort on his part not to shiver, chill air, her touch and the afternoon all together. "Wrong?"

"Think, all right?"

176

"Um." He took the blanket she held out, wrapped in it, and went to the door to get his shirt and soft hat, brought them back to dump in the copper. "That Delegation. Looking!" He came over to the table, sat, still wrapped in the blanket, and set aside the bread and meat she handed him so he could take a good pull of ale. "I thought we decided they would not be looking for me, any more."

"They aren't. Weren't. I don't think." She smiled at him. "Still using your brains, always did like that about you."

"Liked what?" He bit off bread with teeth that were still strong and white, considered her carefully. The lantern was making planes on her face that normally weren't there any more: the years had filled in the hollows in her cheeks, hid the fine, high cheekbones that marked her as foreign the first years here. She was not beautiful, if she ever had been. Unless she smiled.

He didn't often understand what went on behind that smile—or the more usual grave face she presented to the village and to him. Understood less, really, why she'd decided to leave her own company and strike out with him, ten years ago. He'd been held two years beyond his enlistment, *she* had not had any such reason to want to leave; she had been full captain of a mercenary company to his mere sergeant in a large company of horse.

She'd been more, before that: he often forgot—deliberately forgot—she'd been an assassin before she turned mercenary. Forgot even more often that she'd once been a Duke's daughter; she didn't like him to remember that, hadn't liked his knowing it. In truth, that was easier to forget; Liatt hadn't looked like anyone's idea of a Lady at thirty, and now—with ten years of village life under her belt—she looked it even less.

He was still shivering deep in a corner of himself over the afternoon encounter with her; all the years he'd known her, he'd never been—however accidentally—on the business end of those knives. Had never seen her killing face directed toward him.

"Like your brains," Liatt said, bringing him back to the moment. "Villager isn't supposed to have them, nor is an enlisted horse soldier. You had 'em, even then. Used 'em, now and again." She had been smiling, faintly; the smile faded. "No, it's not you, I don't think."

"Don't—"

"Don't interrupt, *I'm* trying to think, it's been too many years since I bothered, and I'm finding it hard work. Why a Delegation here? Why the other things?"

"I thought we decided—"

"You decided, I never did, you know that. You weren't here when the bird came into the barn today. It thrice-circled me, Jahno. It was spying, like the other one."

"Li, by all that's holy—!"

"There isn't much that's holy, Jahno, and listen, will you? Think I didn't make enemies out there? Before I joined the Prince's armies?" Silence. Jahno applied himself to his meat and ale, scowled across the table at her. "Not just an odd enemy, here and there; one or two I lost sleep over. And one lousy wizard. Ever tell you about Kolos?"

"Kolos?" She'd told him damned little, over the

years, but he wasn't about to bring that up just now and miss learning a little more. Liatt would probably take his remark the wrong way, stomp off to tend her pregnant cow and leave him alone the rest of the evening. Then he'd never learn what she was up to. "Not that I recall."

"Used to live in Kalinosa. Just across the sea, in Jaddeh, a little south—"

"Know where Kalinosa is, we almost got sent there, to finish out the Jadders, remember?"

"Well, I lived in Kalinosa—for a while. And I'd been useful to a few people, here and there. So when Kolos decided he needed a certain jewel he sent for me. He *said* it was his, and he wanted it back. Of course, I knew better than that, even then. I presumed it was something he wanted stolen and he was putting a better face on it. He was cautious of his hide, back then. Hadn't the skills then that he started developing later." Her eyes had gone distant; she was eating bread in small bits, washing it down with Jahno's excellent ale, and tasting none of it.

"Skills?" He was more than half afraid he knew what that meant. Her next words confirmed it.

"Sorcerer. Not just nice clean wizardry, but true sorcery. Nasty things, sorcerers, and he was one of the nastier ones, even half trained. Uses toys, spells, charms." She considered that briefly. "He did. As opposed to innate skill or talent. Anyway, that jewel. It was being held by one of the Kalinosan Prelatery, but I got at it." She would have, Jahno thought sourly. "And got it away. But!" She set the wine aside, slid a dagger from some invisible sheath and balanced it on her finger. Jahno pulled his eyes away from it. He had never really liked daggers; he'd learned sword, a little, because they had insisted. He'd spent long hours with a bow, more learning to launch a javelin from a galloping horse. He'd never needed to use short knives, to fight close. The thought made him a little ill.

"I hardly ever fought with them," Liatt said, showing that rare occasional understanding of what *he* was thinking. "Killed, yes. Someone my size doesn't usually get involved in knife fights, my reach is too short and I'm not as strong as a full-grown man, not if he's really trained. You know that, Jahno. I throw them, generally from hiding. Where was I?"

"Kolos," he prompted.

"Kolos. I—I'm no lousy sorcerer, but after a while, you get a feeling for things. I knew he wasn't telling all the truth about the true owner of the jewel, and so it stood to reason he wasn't telling truth about its uses. Just a trifle, he told me; something he needed to set the base of his power, so he could use what he'd learned. I had a friend or two, though: friends I could trust. Damned thing was no more his than it was the Prelatery's; belonged to the temple of Shioh—some fertility thing, to get crops to grow and all that. Nuns and priestesses." Her voice had taken on the usual flat, expressionless tone it bore when she made mention of religion—any religion. "They didn't know what it was capable of, but they had kept it safe for a long time."

"What was it capable of?"

"Don't know. Never heard. What Kolos could have done with it—something unpleasant, I'm sure. The Prelatery had something equally unpleasant in mind. So I relieved them of it, got it back to its original guardians, and tried to impress upon them not to take it out for their field blessings any more." She shrugged gloomily, drank the rest of her ale. "Probably didn't convince them; damned religious think they're exempt from pain and misfortune. Damned goddess didn't protect them first time the jewel got taken, did she?"

"Guess not. What did Kolos do?"

"When he didn't get what he wanted? Probably threw a blue-faced fit and killed a couple of his pretty boys. I know he got my message; I was some days composing it and left it pinned to one of his two-footed pets." She sighed. "I was younger, then, and not very open-minded." She grinned. "Or very sensible, the message I left him was just begging for trouble. But I couldn't resist and besides, I was good and mad. I told him next time to hire a footpad who was also a lackwit, and that I owed him for trying to use me."

"And?"

"And? Oh. Got a message back, eventually, via friends of friends, telling me Kolos was—a little irritated. And that I'd better find another town, perhaps another country, until he cooled off.

"And about a year later, I got a message from Kolos himself. Just that he remembered me, and he remembered the jewel, and when he got the one in his hands, he'd see to the other. And that time was no matter, not to him. You thought *I* could hold a grudge, Jahno." But as he tried to protest, she grinned at him. "Joke, husband." She tipped her mug up, scowled at the dry bottom. Jahno took it from her hand, refilled it, and cut her another chunk of bread. Liatt, unless she had greatly changed, would not dull one of those shining daggers on something so mundane as food. "I think that's what he's done, Jahno. Waited."

"I—oh." Jahno leaned forward, braced his elbows against the table, let his chin drop into his hands, and thought. "I don't know, Li. If it's really him, after you, after all this time—why now?"

"He might only just have found me, there's that. I don't think so, though. I think he just started to look, recently. Because a forty-year-old fighting woman might be easier to kill than a thirty-year-old one. Don't you think?"

He didn't want to ask, but he had to. "So. What—what will you do?"

"Do? Don't know." She slid the dagger back into its pocket; it was gone as though it had never been. She flexed her hands, winced as muscles across her palms and up her forearms protested. "Practice. Be ready. The next move has to be his, doesn't it?" She drank down the rest of the ale, pushed the cup aside and stood. "Right now, though, I'm going to shove that shirt of yours down into the water, go check my cow, and probably try to sleep. I'll be out there with her tonight."

Two days later Liatt killed the demon.

She had been out in the shed earlier, making certain the cow and her twins were doing well; an hour later, terrified bawling and the dog's shrill barking brought her back from the woods at top speed.

It was gloomy inside, and at first she could see nothing but sun-spots; she blinked furiously, moved cautiously into the shade, taking care not to put herself within range of the cow's hooves.

Something was crouched in the far corner, hissing quietly. Kedru was throwing himself against the half-closed door on the house side. That had apparently distracted the thing, or it might have had her before she could see it.

Demon. It was ten years or more since she'd seen one; there was no mistaking the look of it, nor the faint waxy smell that invariably accompanied them. It was hunkered down on three of its four limbs, the long tail curled behind it; the eyes were flat against a flat face, yellow, almost triangular above the mouthful of sharp teeth. It was more snakelike than most; it was waiting for her to make the first move. *Unusual.* But she could play Court Rules, if it could. She saluted it with the left-hand dagger.

"Greetings, slave," she whispered. Kedru's frantic barking nearly covered her voice, but the thing had better ears than that. It smiled at her, exposing an unpleasant number of fangs, and leaned forward.

"Greetings, Nobly Born. Kolos sends his best wishes, and hopes that the years have been good to you." Its offside paw was already going back for a broadside swing at her head when she brought both blades down in an arm's length "X," twisted her wrists once and ripped them through the air in a tee; the knives severed the unseen cords that bound it to the sorcerer's will, and left the demon unmade on the straw at her feet. Messily.

The smell was nearly unbearable; she had forgotten *that,* too. It stopped her thinking, and nearly stopped her breath. *Move the cow, her calves first, get them out into the pen behind the shed. Clean this up.* She shook herself, backed away from the pile of limbs, head and trunk, the blue-green blood that was making the straw sticky. "Li? I heard—ah, gods, what's that smell?" Jahno was in the shed before she could turn to shove him out, before she could even warn him. He caught at her arm, stared down at the thing there, staggered away and lost his breakfast.

"Demon," she said tersely, when he could again hear her. "Out. I'll see to it. Take the cow out, tether her in the shade; the calves will follow."

"I—" He wiped his forehead with a shaky hand. "I'll clean my own mess."

"Never mind. Get the cow out before she does herself harm. Mind her feet!" she added sharply as Jahno came near losing an ear to a flailing hoof. Liatt crossed the small shed to find the spade. It was outside, leaning against the wall, knocked half sideways by the dog. "Go," she ordered it. "It's all right." She drew a deep breath of clean air, held it as she started back toward the mess in the midst of the shed.

It took her five trips, and then another long time to dig the hole for the thing and tip it in, straw and all. Jahno came back through the barn, warily, as she was taking out the separate spadeful of mess that had been his. "I'm sorry."

"Why? I'm surprised I wasn't sick myself, there's not much smells worse than a demon, dead." She carried the last spadeful out, dumped it in the hole and began filling it. "Get back, dog! Nothing here for you!" She glanced at Jahno. "If you want to be of help, get me a couple logs or large stones to set on top; he'll have the thing back out, half eaten and spit up again, otherwise." Jahno blanched, swallowed. Cast a dark look at the pup. Kedru was trying to creep near enough to sample the air, perhaps to get hold of whatever was there, but he was keeping a wary eye on Liatt and that spade.

"Charming habits you've got, thing," Jahno informed the dog sourly, and went in search of weights.

When he got back with the last of them—a chunk of green oak as thick as his waist and as long as his reach that had to be wrestled across the open and into place—Liatt had vanished. He hurried for the house, certain he knew where she'd gone.

It gave him no pleasure to be right. Liatt was kneeling in front of the loft room chest that held all her goods from her former life; on the floor beside her were the heavy breeches with their thick suede reinforcements at knee and seat, the shirt and leather sleeveless jerkin; she was shaking out the corslet as he came up the ladder. It wasn't like his old mail shirt; it was barely mail at all: merely three convex ovals, held together by a small area of reinforced mesh, the whole large enough to cover her heart and not much else. Arrogant mail, he'd called it once. Now it looked pitifully inadequate as well.

"Liatt, you can't go."

She sat back on her heels, her back unyielding, her face and her gaze fixed on the wall. "No? You weren't there for the first crossing in that particular little skirmish. He had Kolos' greeting for me— Kolos' challenge, what it comes down to."

"He'll kill you!"

"He can do that here—and take half this village with him. I wouldn't like that. I've never fit in here, Jahno, but I never have disliked these people. It was never their fault I couldn't be one of them." And because she knew him, knew how his thought went—better than he knew hers—she turned, dropped the armor on top of the jerkin, met his eyes. "Not because of that—what you're thinking. That was another girl, another lifetime. Not me. I wish you'd never known it."

"That you were born noble? Duke's daughter?" She sighed, nodded. "I never think of it, honestly, Liatt!"

"I never give you cause to," she replied tartly, but a corner of her mouth quirked in a smile. "It was all the rest—in between. Most of these women have never set foot beyond the villages. Some of them have scarcely gone beyond this village, I don't think four of them know what the word 'choice' means. I'm nothing like that, you know that. Jahno, by the time I was twenty-two, I'd seen three separate lands, the great sea between them, and killed—well, more men than I can remember." She shrugged, turned back to the chest. "We haven't much in common, the village women and I. Or the men, come to that. Save you—before you start to worry."

"I don't," he said quietly, but he did, and she knew he did. "But you can't just go off looking for this Kolos, Liatt!"

"I won't be 'just looking.' I have a fair notion where he might be. He wants me, Jahno. He'll see that I find him. But I have to go. You can see that."

"I can't." But that was stubbornness. And so was the other thought, though he knew well enough how she'd answer that one: "I'll go with you, then."

"No. That isn't sense, Jahno. It's not your fight."

"I can't let you just go!"

"Jahno, there was an oath between us, once, do you remember?" She hadn't raised her voice at all, but it overrode his easily. "No holds upon each other, the way folk put holds upon each other when they wed? None of this 'protect and protected' trash, and no fighting of each other's battles. I remember it, Jahno. Oath, remember it?"

"This isn't—"

"Kolos is my matter, not yours."

"Liatt—damn all!" he shouted suddenly, his face bright red. "There's this cow of yours, there's the rest of the garden to get in and dry! There's—how am I to do all that myself, and with Madda's harvest as well?" Silence. "And what of *that*? You show yourself seldom enough out in the village, but it won't be a day before folk know you're gone! What do I tell them?"

"Whatever you wish," Liatt said coolly. She brought out dark, heavy boots, eyed them dubiously. Her feet hadn't been encased in anything so ungiving as that in years, they would be uncomfortable indeed. "Tell them I went to visit my mother."

Jahno laughed sourly. "I might as well admit I killed you and buried the body under that log out back! Remember Ridian, two falls ago?"

Liatt turned to eye him with amusement. "I doubt anyone in *this* village will think you killed me! Now, if you were to vanish, Jahno, they might start combing the woods for marks of new burial."

"Very amusing, Liatt!" He was seething, more with indignation than anything else, knowing the battle lost and her already gone in thought if not otherwise. "They'll know you've put on man's garb and gone gadding in search of war again; they'll say the Prince's Delegation made you hungry for your old ways again, and I'll be unable to show my face in any of the taverns in the area! They'll laugh me right out the door! And Madda, gods, what will Madda think?"

"The worst, as ever," Liatt replied imperturbably. She fished in the boots rather gingerly, evicted a spider from one, pulled out the wool foot wrappings she'd stored in the toes. Sniffed cautiously. She *had* washed them before storing them, and they appeared to be whole still. The heavy cloak under had one small hole in the shoulder, and there was no time to patch it, but with good luck she'd have no need of shelter from rain. It she did—well, a little rain hurt no one. "Madda never has been pleased with me as a daughter, this will at least give her new fuel for her nasty tongue."

"Li, that's unfair!"

"Jahno, you know her better than I, and you know yourself she wasn't sorry to see you slink home to hide and the inn go to your brother instead of you!" That stopped him a moment; he knew, and hated knowing. "I'm sorry."

"Never *mind* that! Liatt, by all the little green tree-gods, you can't do this! You're too old to go haring off on some fool quest."

Her hands froze in midair over the chest; she let her head fall to one side, finally turned to look at him. "I'm forty. That's old enough to know better than damn fool quests. This isn't one. The damn fool part was when I was still young and brash, and I should have given Kolos his wretched stone or killed him, and I did neither. So call it a bad choice. Or think of it that I'm merely paying a debt. No," she added as he opened his mouth to speak again. "Don't offer again. You can't go in my place, you can't go with me. You reminded me of all that needs keeping up around here; you're better suited to that than I, and I have a trick or two up my sleeve for Kolos that you don't have."

"Knives?" he asked tiredly.

"A thing or two I learned, besides fighting and killing. A spell or two, a special wizard's trick of my own." She went back to the chest, felt its bottom carefully. "Jahno?" The suddenly quiet voice made him nervous indeed; he'd been waiting for this moment since he'd come flying across the yard and through the door, up the ladder.

"Um—Liatt?"

"Jahno, where is my sword?"

"Um—sword?" Her back was still to him; she'd gone very still indeed. It took the greatest effort he could put to it, to keep his mouth shut and not babble inanities.

"It was here, in the bottom of his chest, and not that long ago, Jahno. Where is it?"

There was no getting around it. He sighed. "At the inn. Above the mantle, along with mine. Eghen thought the walls needed something, when he heard the Delegation was on its way, and there was no time to whitewash, no time for banners—" His voice faded as Liatt shut the chest, gently indeed, and turned around to sit, cross-legged, next to her fighting gear. She looked, suddenly, very tired.

"Jahno. Dear, sweet Jahno. Do you know what you've done? That sword of mine—*my* sword, by the way—is unusual. Unique, maybe. Remember me telling you about it? Yours is like any other blade, anyone's anywhere. But mine! You might as well have sent Kolos an engraved note from me, telling him where I was!"

"No!" he protested faintly. She was piling things in her arms, heading toward the ladder with purpose. He backed down ahead of her, held it as she descended with both arms full. She dropped the load on the table, leaned against it, eyes closed.

"If I had known what you did—no matter. Once they saw that blade, it was bound to get out I was here. No doubt he was already looking for me, and that just helped speed things up. If one of that Delegation is Kolos' man—I told you about the bird?" He nodded, realized she wasn't watching him.

"You told me."

"So he's a few days ahead of me, but not many." She fixed him with a cold, appraising look. "You'll have to get that blade back from Eghen for me. Now." He opened his mouth, shut it again, Liatt, as sensitive as ever to his expressions, laughed sourly. "Don't tell me. Let me guess. You *gave* him the blades, yours and mine, free gift. That right? Because they weren't being used—"

"I didn't think—"

"I can see that! Gods. Worse by the moment! Get me some ale, will you, husband? And let me try to think myself!" She dropped into her chair. *Husband*, Jahno thought grimly as he brought the cup and shoved it into her hands. *That may be a good sign, she hasn't yet cast me off for good and all.* Not that it mattered, if she went out on this quest; that sorcerer would carve her up, leave a little pile of bits and pieces—like that thing he sent. Jahno remembered that suddenly, and all too clearly. He swallowed hard, went for ale for himself.

"Anyone else, I could say it was a mistake and ask it back," Liatt was musing aloud. "Your brother, though—bad enough that I would be taking back a gift you made, but that it's my sword, a woman's sword—" She grinned faintly, very briefly. "He'd have a such a fit, your nephews would inherit your inn much too young, wouldn't they?" Jahno closed his eyes and buried his face in his cup. "So I'll have to steal it back," Liatt concluded gloomily, but there was a light in her eyes that Jahno caught as he sat up and stared across the table at her.

"They'll catch you, Liatt!"

"Hah." She finished her ale, shoved the cup away. "I was a thief when your brother was still at Madda's breast! Well—maybe not *quite*," she amended carefully. "Why not? I'll wager you they don't even notice the blade is gone if you don't tell them. And their guard dog—I trained Khia myself, what's to worry? Besides. If I'm gone, what can they do?"

Jahno shook his head. "What are you going to do for a horse? You can't take ours, I'm sorry, Li, I need her here. You know I do."

"I won't need one."

"You'll be a year and a half getting through the woods on foot!"

"Not necessarily." And, diffidently, "I'm a Stairmaker. That—well." She looked almost embarrassed. "It was what they gave me, those nuns, after I brought back their wretched jewel." She reached to grip Jahno's hand hard. "Don't look at me like that! I didn't just grow an extra ear or something, did I? It's only herb magic, not true sorcery, you know."

Stairmaker? It took his breath, left him speechless. There were some pretty wild tales in the east, where he'd done most of his fighting. Where there were still a lot of wizards of one kind or other. So many, they had regulating guilds, just like tradesmen, or so it was said. Magic like Stairmaking was rare. At least, he'd never seen it. It took certain herbs and spells, they said, so that a man or woman could make steps up onto the air, as though it were formed and solid as stairs. Once at a certain height above trees and rivers and towns, supposedly they could then stride with the clouds, walking faster than a man could run. He'd never exactly believed in Stairmakers, it just didn't sound possible. And now—his Liatt?

Not his, if she'd ever been. At the moment he felt reft indeed; the woman who had shared his blankets and his house for ten years, who'd fed him and been fed by him, who'd fought poverty and adversity with him—shorn of his birthright and even his name as he'd had to be—until they'd eked out a modest living and even a bit of comfort in this small end of the kingdom, that woman was gone. A stranger sat across from him, holding his fingers and gazing at him with grave concern, but she was already half on her journey, planning herself away from him. Planning to fight a sorcerer with sorcerer's tools. He hadn't realized how much he wanted her, until he'd watched her make her choice and lost her.

"I'd better be gone, soon. Before Kolos finds another demon and sends it. The next one might not fail; this one was overfull of its own strength and thought to gloat first. Next time, I might not be able to make both passes before it attacks. You'd be burying me for certain then, Jahno; if I didn't have to bury you instead." Her fingers tightened briefly on his, let them go. "I wouldn't care for that."

To his horror, he felt tears welling up. He swallowed, sniffed hard, and when he spoke his voice was harsh. "You're determined on it, go then! But I'm damned by every god there is if you're leaving that rotten dog with me!"

It was nearer dawn than not when Liatt stole out of the bed she and Jahno shared, shivering a little in the chill air. She dressed quickly and quietly, one eye on the hump of body against the wall, though she hadn't much real worry that Jahno might waken: she'd dosed his last cup of ale when he wasn't looking. He snored gently. She sniffed quietly, rubbed a hand over her damp eyes, and tiptoed over to the hearth to sit and wind the woolen strips snugly around her feet. The boots would be tight with them, but miserable without: she couldn't afford blisters. The boots *were* tight, but not unbearably so. The shirt was the worst, snug across the breasts, but the leather jerkin laced up the sides and was no problem. She stuffed the armor inside her cloak.

Jahno gave no sign of waking as she pulled back the heavy wool blanket and kissed his brow. She tiptoed across the room, gathered her pack, her old hat, the cloak, and moved silently through the door. It squeaked a little as she drew it toward her, and Jahno mumbled in his sleep, flopped over onto his back.

Out in the yard, she set her things down and considered. Finally shrugged. It was no more than an hour till dawn and she wanted to be well into the woods, out into the clearing where Jahno and his cousins were felling trees for next winter's fires. She'd need a clear space the size of that to start; it had, after all, been ten years since she'd Built. And she'd have Kedru, who would doubtless be a problem.

So there would be no time to make two trips of it. The dog came up and sat beside her, yawned hugely. "All right," she whispered. "You come. But quiet!" She hefted her pack, his, gathered the cloak to her and started off toward the village square.

The inn lay in a pool of shadow, the windows above it where the household and any paying guests slept all dark. She sat on the stoop, tugged off her boots, dropped them on the stack of gear and caught the dog by the ruff. "Guard," she hissed against his ear. Kedru sat still enough; she could only hope the word sank in and that he'd stay put and keep still.

It was even darker inside, but there was a faint glow of embers under a thick gray coating of ash; that guided her across the room. Someone had put the benches back against the wall when they closed up for the night; that was in her favor, at least. Khia came up from in front of the hearth, sniffing; she shoved her long nose in Liatt's hand, whimpering faintly, but was obediently silent at a gesture. The sword was there, out of her reach, but a cautiously moved bench took care of that. She only just remembered to replace the bench after she buckled the sword where it belonged—

she didn't really want Jahno to have to put up with any more misery from his callous family. She doubted Eghen would notice his missing decor for some time to come.

For a wonder, Kedru was still standing guard over her goods, and silently at that. Nor did he whine a greeting when she emerged from the doorway, he merely attached himself to her side as she put her boots back on, gathered things up, and set out for the western road in a ground-eating stride. They reached the narrow trail in short order, followed it by the first gray-blue light to the cut clearing where Jahno had been felling.

It was never pretty, such a logged site in the midst of tall forest; at this hour, it was ugly indeed: trees down and dying, a huge and daily growing pile of ends, limbs and branches for folk to come picking through themselves—nothing to burn a proper fire or hold it the night, but plenty of kindling to start one. The ground was torn up, rough lines shorn through grass and bramble to bare dirt, where oxen or horses had been hooked to lines, to pull the logs over to the tall curing stacks.

She dismissed it, then: a necessary evil. They needed firewood, and by the following summer, the clearing would have a rough beauty all its own. She found a place near the clearing's western edge, where the sun would strike first, and settled in to wait for that hour. In the meantime, there was still gear to don, to store, and Kedru's pack.

The dog was not at all agreeable to wearing the cloth and leather bag she'd fashioned for his mother, some years before; she had to cuff him into submission before he'd stand still for it, and even then he kept turning his head to try and pull it off, or bending down to try to get his teeth under the chest strap. He'd stop that if he actually caught hold of it: Michat got her lower jaw stuck under the strap once and never tried to pull it off that way again.

Liatt cuffed him again, made him lay down, and brought out the daggers, dropped sword and belt long enough to distribute them over her body. She had to again leave the chest baldric in the pack because the knives would be unusable, even if she could get them and the shirt both around her. The small bit of armor went on next: it was bronze, old but well forged and finely worked. Not that she'd needed it, very often. It protected what needed it most, though, and weighed considerably less than the ring stuff Jahno had had to fight in.

The sword next: She felt the old tingle of something that might have been apprehension, the upsurge of pleasure that quickened her heart as she grasped the hilt and drew it. It wasn't a particularly fancy thing, no snotty lord's party jewelry. More likely, given the size and fine cut of it, it had been crafted for a noble's son, not the practice blade he'd wield under a tutor, but the one he'd wear as normally as he'd wear breeches. There were two nice gems tucked in the fancy work on the hand guard, and the fancy work was inlaid with silver. But the blade itself was a wonder: light, well-forged, truly balanced, and polished to a glorious sheen even now, unused as it had been for so long.

She could not have said at the time what drew

her to it, when she wangled it out of that Lady's hands—family trove, the Lady had said, she'd had no right to get rid of it, but Liatt had insisted, and an honor debt was after all an honor debt. The sheath had held a decent handful of gold coin; the Lady had been generous once persuaded. Of course, against what she'd nearly lost—honor, dowry and life all at once—a family antique and a purseful of gold wasn't much matter.

But the sword *had* called itself to her attention. Liatt was certain of that. She was less certain—but suspected—that it had little tricks, almost a mind or a life of its own. It somehow eased aches and pains, the small agonies a fledgling swordswoman should have felt during training, for this blade had been her first and only sword. If it wasn't the sword, there wasn't much other explanation for the lack of stiffness she'd had, taking up its use. She hoped it was the sword: such a gift would stand a middle-aged and unpracticed swordswoman in good stead.

Another thing she could not prove: she was certain the hilt had guided her hand to the proper parry, the necessary thrust, more than once, in those early days. It could have been skill; she doubted that, remembering her first lessons.

It had one trick that was construction, not magic or supposition; one even the noblewoman had not known. Liatt pulled it from its sheath, ran a fond hand down the blade, then turned it sideways and pressed the two small, dark studs on either side of the cross-grip. The stiletto shot out the end of the pommel, a hand's length of wicked death set into the end of the grip. Another stud, a little harder to find, sent it back into place again.

She'd used that twice, when sword skill had failed her and it had gone to a close fight.

Her small bag of coin—she hefted it. Money from her cattle breeding, the calves, the dogs she'd sold over the past year or so. None of it gold, but enough good silver to get them passage over the Salten Sea, if she got so far.

She'd have to take passage, too: She couldn't walk over water. The nuns said someone truly virtuous might do that, and she was far from that. She'd be fortunate if she could manage to get the Stair high enough to reach walking altitude over the Greatwood, even more fortunate if it worked out above the northern desert. Winds, heat, sand, all did odd things to it: the Way itself was usually stable once the Stair got to the right level above ground, but it could be tricky in the wrong places. And if Kolos was waiting out there in his desert fastness, he might make it difficult for her just for the fun of it.

She couldn't be certain Kolos was still there, but it was the best place she knew to look. Of course, there might be word of him in the port cities along the Sea, which was really only a large inlet from the main sea.

Likely she would not have to look for him at all, of course. Like she'd told Jahno, Kolos had wanted her attention, he'd make certain she found him.

After a moment's thought, she sheathed the blade, settled the baldric in place a little better, and fished out a length of stout cord. One end got a loop, which she wound in leather strapping, the other went around Kedru's neck. Just at the moment, she wasn't so pleased herself, thinking about mounting the air and walking above the trees; the dog wasn't going to enjoy it at all. She eyed him tiredly, inwardly cursing Jahno for his stubbornness and the dog for his brainlessness. The pup looked up at her from his resting place, his tail thumped hopefully. She clomped him roughly on the top of his head, driving his ears down, but they came right back up and he grinned at her, panting quietly. "Damn fool dog," she said. The dog twisted its head, licked her hand, and she ruffled his neck.

It was growing light, and sun touched the tops of the trees just above their heads. Time to start; she had to be up and gone before the men came out here to work, and that would not be long after sunrise. She fished in her belt pouch, drew out the tiny packet of fine suede, its gold leaf markings scarcely faded. She elbowed the dog aside when he would have sniffed it, laid it on the log behind her, and carefully unfolded it. The incense cake was pungent, one corner barely singed, the thin-coated bit of linen paper under it untouched by the ash or the dark rose of the cake. She dragged out flint and tinder, lit the corner, unfolded the bit of paper. One finger held the loose, dry contents of that paper in place—a tiny aspen leaf, a single airborne seed from a faded liontooth, the twisted winged seed from a maple—while she read the contents. That took time, it had been long since she'd made sense of the complex marks on paper. *Too long. I used to read for the pleasure of it, I've buried myself alive in this place.*

She shook her head sharply, refolded the paper, bent her head to sniff the rising thread of smoke. It filled her, left her momentarily light-headed, then jubilant as after a third cup of old wine at midsummer night. *Giddy*, she admonished herself, but it was the stuff itself at work as much as a sudden upsurging of freedom. She inhaled a second time, then brought the dog's head close. Kedru struggled only briefly, sat back licking his chops as she snuffed the incense block with the bit of suede wrapping. Ready. Or as ready as she could get. Sun was most of the way down the trees, it would touch her head in a moment, when she stood. She rewrapped the packet, stowed it in the pouch at her belt.

Sun warmed her face, her hands. She draped the dog's rope over a branch on the fallen log, and ordering him to stay put, murmured "Ayetha. Lidaw. Esham." She lifted her right foot, slowly lowered it. It stopped before it touched ground, nearer her left knee than not. A glow wrapped her; she shut it away, fearing the least intrusion into the building of the Stair. This was the difficult part; once she reached height, maintaining it should be no hardship at all. Kedru whined faintly. "Shut," she ordered. He subsided but eyed her anxiously as she brought the left foot up to join the right. "Ayetha. Lidaw. Esham." A second step, faintly shimmering in the first rays of morning sun. It took her weight as though it were stone. She built three more before she went back for the dog. She had the feel of it now, the confidence she could continue to construct it—another twenty steps or more, the forest ran tall here—even with the distraction.

"Kedru. Come." She felt her way back down to the first step. Kedru whined again and went flat on his belly, muzzle flat in the dirt, ears down;

brown eyes gazed at her in open fear. She sighed. Crouched. "Kedru." The dog absolutely refused to move; he could have tugged the lead free but wasn't about to if it meant going where Liatt was. She came back down to solid ground, slid her hand through the loop. "Come." He might have been part of the undergrowth, he eyed her mournfully but would not move. "Bless all the gods at once, you're still young and not full weight yet," she growled, and scooped him up in strong arms.

Kedru struggled wildly. He subsided as she freed a hand long enough to cuff him one. "Hold still!" He eyed her sidelong, licked his chops and pressed against her.

It was awkward, building steps, speaking the words, balancing the dog who—if he no longer fought her—was still enough of a weight to throw her off balance. Once she had the tenth step solid under them, it came a bit easier; that was partly because of the full sun on her, partly the least of breezes that soughed through the trees and ruffled her hair, set Kedru's thick ruff to tickling her upper lip. Partly practice: it might not have been ten years, for the ease she was having. By the twentieth step, she was constructing them almost as fast as she could pace them.

They reached the tops of the trees without incident. Liatt walked off the Stair, crouched momentarily on the Way itself, set a shivering Kedru at her feet, and with a quietly spoken "Leshan" unmade the Way behind her. The village was still in shade, Jahno might just now be wakening to a bed only half warm and her parting note: "Love, Liatt. I'll return." Short of necessity: she couldn't think of words to console him that she would feel easy writing, and he wasn't much lettered anyway. And all she'd had for materials was the table top and a bit of blackened wood from the fireplace.

It was a clear, cloudless morning, late summer: that was in her favor. The Greatwood looked odd from this perspective: trees in all directions, shading away toward the tundra and ice-fields many days' ride south. North it grew ever darker and thicker; here and there mountains or a tall line of hills showed. Mostly forest. Even from this perspective, she could not see desert—it was too far distant—and the sea was cut off to the west by the Coastal Range. The peaks of some of those were still snowclad, even so late in the season; their own stream was fed by that snow.

The wind was picking up, here above the trees, and the sun was warm on her right cheek as she started north.

Kedru fought her at first, nervous about setting his feet down where he could see nothing to hold them up. Liatt kept her eyes resolutely fixed on the north horizon. It had never been one of her favorite vistas, down from a floorless height, and the speed at which they moved dizzied her if she saw the tree tops flowing past her feet. She continued to have her hands full with the young dog, once he regained his confidence: he discovered birds below them, and now and again squirrels in the tops of trees, chattering furiously at the intruders.

The leash held him, but it instilled no sense in him. One squawk from something small and fast-moving had him lunging, Liatt half off her feet, and it took what seemed forever to get him to stop.

They camped the first night deep in the woods, in a small clearing it had taken Liatt some time to find: but she needed an open place to descend, as well as to ascend from the next morning. Fortunately, there was water nearby; she'd carried a water bottle and there was a second in the dog's pack, but she hated drinking stale, warm water unless absolutely necessary.

Kedru was nearly as worn as she from the distance they had covered, and it was only the dog's presence that kept her awake long enough to make a fire and feed them both. She flexed her hands as she waited for her tea to steep: they were still stiff, but not unbearably so, and her grip was much stronger. Gods, it had *had* to be, fighting that fool of a dog most of the day!

She took his pack off and scratched his back for him, then turned him loose, unworried that he might run off: in such unfamiliar surroundings, he wouldn't be likely to desert the one thing known to him.

Food revived her a little; enough that she was able to go back to the stream to wash. The chill of the water brought her a little more awake, and she drew the sword, went through a full series of practice maneuvers that had been her first exercises with it. She was surprised at her dexterity; over the years she'd lived with Jahno she'd scarcely touched the daggers and the sword not at all, fearing at first to bring it out and give herself away, later having no time for it and still not wanting to stir up gossip and renewed speculation about her past—in a village where there were few secrets. She'd kept most of hers, and had intended to go on keeping them.

She hadn't even thought of passes and sets and exercises, any more than she'd thought of targets and slender blades to pierce them—but her arms and her fingers had remembered a lot of it for her.

One thing certain, though; she'd have to part with a little of her coin, once she got to Urfu, for a sparring partner. She hadn't the speed she would need, and fighting against air was no way to prepare to fight Kolos' killers. She didn't dare chance that he wouldn't have armsmen, or wouldn't send them against her.

"What a waste," she grouched into her tea. When she first dealt with him, Kolos had surrounded himself with expert swordsmen, all young, male and wonderful to look at. Two of those she'd sent to an early reckoning had quickened *her* pulse, or would have under better circumstances. Possibly she'd have quickened theirs, too; Kolos bought his boys for looks and form—not with any eye to their preferences.

"Pretty boys. Ah, well. Times change. Ten years and I've bedded the same man every night, there's a change indeed." Kedru's ears perked up at the sound of her voice; he came across from the place he'd taken next to the small fire and shoved his nose hard against her arm. "And so tonight I bed down with an idiot child of a dog. Turn for the better, eh?" Kedru's tail thumped once, he wriggled, shoved harder until his nose pushed between her elbow and her ribs. She hugged him, laughed. The sound was dampened by trees all around them. "Better than many a one I've had, willing or otherwise, dog."

She gave him a shove, tossed the last dregs of

her tea out into the darkness, banked the small fire and stood to pull her cloak around her shoulders. "Come." He snuggled down with his chin on her knee, unused to such liberties but willing to take advantage if she was willing to permit. "Guard," she added, and breathed a brief silent prayer to the jewel's goddess that either her own inner ear was still sharp, or that the dog might for once pay heed.

Or better still—that there be no need for guard at all.

There were three more days of such travel, and she woke that first morning so stiff from the unaccustomed exertion and from sleeping on the hard ground that it took an extra hour to get herself upright, and to walk out the worst of it on the ground before she could construct the Stairway. Kedru gave her no trouble after that first day, at least so far as the Stairway and the Walking itself were concerned, though he cared even less for his second and third whiffs of the incense. And he was still inclined to chase after anything small enough to run or fly from him.

The second day they walked far indeed, all the way to the lower slopes of Dragon Height itself, for she could find no clearing nearer than the meadows along its southern face. The ground was unrelievedly rocky under an all-too-thin carpet of grass and tiny flowers, but near the edge of the woods she found ripe berries. Kedru promptly slobbered all over the lower branches and proceeded to clear them of ripe and partially ripe fruit, leaving her only the upper, but there were more than enough for her and the swarms of hornets chewing on the overripe berries. She fed him a handful of fruit, pulled stray thorns out of his muzzle, and filled one of the water bottles with all the berries she could fit into it

The wide open slope was chilly sleeping, for a constant wind blew down from the snow-capped heights, piercing her cloak with ease. But the sun hit her much earlier than it had the morning before, and the Stairway went up the few steps needed to reach the Way with no effort at all.

The detour it took to bring her around the Dragon served to wake her muscles, and it was a pleasant walk. Kedru went frantic only once, nearly pulling her over when he saw a bear making its way up the scree-strewn slabbed heights, but he came back into line readily enough when she yelled at him.

That evening, as they came down into a wide meadow at the side of a broad, shallow river, she thought she could see the inland sea, and beyond that, the gleam of pale gold that was desert.

Late afternoon the day after saw them at the edge of the woods. The river curved away east and was lost in bogs and marshes, one branch following the path that came out of the northern border of Greatwood. It led to a narrow, roughly constructed bridge that clattered under her feet, and thence to a small, half-walled town—not really much above a village but with pretensions to higher status.

A guard, in bright colors and polished bronze breastplate, stood at the end of the bridge. The town elders might not have been able to afford him sword-lessoning—that was the usual reason for staves and pikes—but his pike was a good one, well forged with its heavy central thrusting blade and flanking, fluted, winglike slashing side blades, intricately patterned and enameled. Three bright banners fluttered just below the *corsik* blade. That style of *corsik* had been dated when Liatt first took up her knives, and so had no doubt been bought used by the town for its guard. Fashionable or not, it could still kill.

The pike came down in front of her, barring the way. She tugged the dog to a sit at her side. "I'm from the south, come to trade."

"Trade? What for what?"

"Is that not my business? Or has the border hereabouts gone dangerous these past years?"

He eyed her in silence. Shrugged finally, and pulled the pike aside. "Not here, not yet anyway. There's been trouble across—there," he jerked his head toward the salt water, its north shores. "You've come here to Virith before?"

"Once, a long time since. I have coin to trade for passage to Urfu, and for meat and a room for myself and my dog tonight."

"Coin." He was thoughtful a moment. She fought a rising anger at the look he gave her, knowing the thought that went with it. Village woman, peasant. Middle years, and more than usually plain. Shapeless under that concealing cloak, doubtless, or she'd not dare wear men's breeches in a town. "The City leaders would not like me to say such things to a visitor to Virith, but a woman and alone—well, a word to your ear. The dog looks no more than a pup, and seems not much guard for you. If you have coin, I would show little of it; there's a rascal or two within the walls."

Or several hundreds, if Virith is half the waterfront town it once was. "Thank you for the warning, I'll use care," she said and strode on past him, Kedru in close tow. She wondered briefly what the guard would have thought if she'd sprung a knife on him. *Pity the poor rascal who thinks to separate me and my coin, if you want to pity anyone,* she thought back at him.

There was, finally, a room; she'd sensibly insisted upon a window too small for a man to breach, shutters that barred, and a door with a bolt. "Amazing, dog; I felt less afraid out in the woods," she told Kedru when they were finally locked in. The room itself was neat and the bedding reasonably clean—it needed shaking, but she'd expected worse. The bar and common room below had been rough and wild even before the sun went down, and it cost her an extra two coins to have food for them both brought to the room. And this was the tamest of four inns she'd tried.

A rascal or two: more than that. The Prince's Dispensers of Justice were wasting their time on small villages, they were needed here. She grinned, just thinking of those five middle-aged men, trying to imagine them sitting down in the public room below to enforce the Prince's law.

The innkeeper's daughter came with meat and bread, both hot; a dark red tuber steaming where it had been cut open, melted white cheese and herbs spilling down its thick skin. Two tankards of ale and another of water. "So you do not have to come to the railing to call for more ale, Lady," the girl explained. Liatt gave her an extra small copper coin for herself, and got in return information on how to reach the docks, where she would seek transport across to Urfu. And an inn in Urfu, a keeper Liatt could trust, with the girl's name and her father's to make certain of a welcome.

She found it hard to sleep that night, for all the noise below, and then for the silence—the creaking of boards and settling of a house not hers, and a bed not hers. For the very stillness and stuffiness of the air. Even with two large mugs of ale in her—ale that was inferior even to Eghen's.

She did sleep, finally. But that was no comfort, for Kolos was awaiting her there. *So. I flushed you from your hiding place, Nobly Born.*

That title is not mine, she retorted furiously, *and there was no hiding place where I was, was there?"*

The laugh shuddered through her; near black, keen eyes quested for hers. He was clean shaven where he'd been bearded, but the reason for that was visible in the hair that was as much gray as black. *Vain bastard.* Lack of beard made him look no younger, though; the lines around his mouth, those running down into his jaw, all showed. And the weak chin that had been responsible for the original beard. *You do not meet my gaze, Nobly Born; is that polite?*

If I could make it less polite, I would. I was comfortable where I was. You spoiled that.

He laughed again, loud and long; beside her thrashing, twisting body, Kedru licked his lips and whimpered. *Ever polite, Nobly Born! You have not changed, have you? Except,* he added with silken malice, *that you are older now.*

Trust to that, if it pleases you.

Perhaps I shall. A word of advice, however.

Waste no more time than you have; I am older also, and it has made me impatient. He was gone; Liatt rolled over and was uncomfortably, nervously awake.

She closed her eyes a moment, fought air in and out of her lungs. Kedru edged up the bedding, thrust his head against her hand. She started, realized what it was and let the hand stay where it was. Slowly, much too slowly, her pulse came back to normal. She made herself get up, then, lit the candle on the small table next to the wash basin. She went to the window, silently, one hand motioning the dog to stay put. She listened intently, then finally opened the casement and gazed out across roofs to the forest and a westering moon.

She bolted the window again, then wandered over and checked the door. Finally she returned to the bed and sat on its edge. "Nightmare, dog. Shouldn't have let it get under my skin like that, though. Maybe I am getting old." Kedru's ears came up briefly; he nudged his way under her hand. She grinned, ruffled his head and got up to blow the candle out. Kedru let her get comfortable; then positioned himself hard at her back. Jahno-like. Well, but he wasn't Jahno, and not half the comfort when she woke shaking and terrified from some evil dream, afraid to so much as put her feet to the floor or to go in search of light, lest something be there and take her. Wretched puppy was better by far than nothing, though. She heard him draw one deep, snorting breath that was half snore, grinned faintly and closed her eyes. It was past sunrise when she opened them again.

* * *

The docks reeked of fish; there'd been a catch the previous morning and the town's screeching collection of gulls and rooks hadn't quite cleaned up all the orts down on the sand and gravel under the wooden planks. For one who'd been so long away from docks and fish, the stench was a constant threat to the peace of her breakfast, but urgency beyond the prior night's dreams moved her. She had to find a ferry, today if possible, tomorrow at latest. A ferry that would take her around the eastern end of the lake and up to Urfu.

She chafed at the news—at least a two-day journey in an elderly boat. But the boats she'd counted on, the sleek sailing ships that had once plied the twenty leagues straight across the Sea between Virith and Urfu were eight years gone. What boats still sailed from Urfu and Virith could not cross the Sea in a single day, and none of the captains was fool enough to try it in two. Out of sight of land, north and south, a man could lose direction, and storms had begun to come with disturbing suddenness the past few years.

No choice. She'd have to take one of the tubby little cayeeks, with its twin rudders, its pair of triangular sails. They were slow, the distance much greater. There'd be a stop or two for the nights along the shore. She chafed at the waste of time, knowing all the same that there was no faster alternative; she could not walk the Sea and by horse it would take her three times as long to come to Urfu by skirting the Sea and the marshes along its shores.

There were three ferries, or so the landlord's

daughter had told her, running the passage on offset days: *Killdeer* should be on its way back from the north, and *Wave* might not be long behind, if replacement sails were to be had. She'd sent word back with *Tradewind* on its last run; her sails had been old and had made their last passage; heavy winds had shredded the mainsail and blown holes in the jib.

Which meant, in effect, that there was only *Tradewind*. Liatt lounged back in shadow a while, watching as Nikosan and his young crewman unloaded crates and jars of oil encased in wooden frames, as he jested with the tradesmen's servants who were waiting for the goods. He and the boy—a nephew too young for beard and barely to man's height—took on cargo, then the boy was ordered forward to work on the rigging.

Two men came up while they were unloading and loading to speak to Nikosan; one of these went away grumbling and scowling after long and hard argument. The second—a tall man in a soldier's cloak—paid coin for his passage and concluded the deal with a handshake. Only Liatt saw the look on his face as he turned away from the little cayeek to go for his bags and his blankets: he kept the hand away from his clothing, wiped it on the rough boards of the shed she leaned against, was gone. Apparently Nikosan was no cleaner than he looked. The landlord's daughter had warned her about that, but said he was trustworthy.

Well, one didn't preclude the other, she'd been around men cleaner than sacrificial lambs who were low, and the village tanner was one of the most honest she'd ever met—though she couldn't bear to be downwind of him unless he'd bathed.

She stretched, tugged on the dog's rope and crossed the planking. "Shipsmaster. Passage to Urfu—how much?"

He registered the voice before he saw her; was grinning as he turned. What he saw—small, past youth and alone—widened the grin. "For yourself? No coin." It had been too long; it took her a moment to understand what he meant. For one half-insane moment, she found herself considering it. Common sense reasserted itself as quickly: *You aren't half so short on coin as that! And you have Jahno, could you ever explain to him you traded passage for half the captain's bed? Would you want to try? Gods, she'd never want him to know!*

Nikosan had seen the half-thought intention and was grinning at her. She closed the small distance between them, a short blade already in each hand. One touched his chin, gently. "Perhaps you'd reconsider, boatsman? I, myself, would not wish to chance sleeping with a woman whose first companions are daggers. Indeed, I would not wish even to annoy her."

Assassin. It registered in his face with almost comic dismay. He swallowed. "N-n-no insult, not intended, swear it!"

"None taken. The price?" she urged as he would have backed away from her. She slid the blades back out of sight. He named one: three copper, one silver. She laughed sourly, countered. This was firmer ground, and though she hadn't bargained with his like in some years, she'd honed her skills in the village and at the multi-village markets. They finally settled on one silver, a copper extra if she wanted his cooking both nights. A corner of the deck for her and the dog to sleep. Liatt, after another glance around the deck of the ferry, decided to feed herself.

He held out a hand. She took it, returned the hard pressure. "Be aboard in an hour; I won't wait." Nikosan was already halfway up the battered plank before she could reply, shouting orders at the boy who was half-tangled in ropes and yelling for his help. *Gods*, Liatt thought disgustedly, and scrubbed her palm on her breeches; it wasn't as blackened as it felt, just oily and gritty. *I'd have had to throw him in the lake and soaped him before I could have borne to touch him!* Picturing that lightened her mood considerably.

"By Xirian's golden bells, it's never Liatt!" A voice brought her around, hands catching at the daggers again, but they stayed hidden. The earlier passenger had returned with his belongings and a friend—a friend whose voice and face were familiar. He laughed, let his free hand drop to her shoulder, and gave it a shake. "There was never but one woman of such size with that hair and that stance! Gods, it's years and I knew you halfway across the docks by the back and all that dark hair! Holy Xirian, you've been gone from sight so long, I thought you dead!" She couldn't get a word in edgewise; stood instead smiling at him doubtfully and trying to match a name to that strong, tanned face. "Jahno—you and he left together, how is he? Or do you know?"

"Married to him ten years," she said in the space he finally left her. He goggled at her. Her tentative smile became a grin; she had him now, by that silly pop-eyed face. "Stop that, Elgan! Or should I say—Elegance himself, as ever, aren't you?"

"Married! Never have thought it! Our Liatt?"

"Yours, hah!" she retorted. "I wasn't your *anything*, Elegance, my sweet!"

"Well—the company's Liatt, and you can't deny you were that! Captained us, two battles running, when Vikro died, didn't you?" He dropped his bundles, caught at his companion and dragged him forward. "Wurghen, I've told you about her often enough. Liatt." She found herself shaking hands with the second man, who had been watching her warily as she and Elgan talked. "My friend Wurghen—shake the lady's hand, don't be offensive, lad!"

"Don't you 'lady' *me*, Elgan! And what lies have you been telling the man? Look at his face! I don't bite, Wurghen," she added tartly as she retrieved her fingers. "And as for Jahno—well, someone had to keep him from trouble, didn't they?"

"I suppose. He always had a nose for it. Or a talent, whichever you like." He gripped her shoulder again and hugged her hard. "You look like a woman with a mission. Where are you bound? Any cause we can help with?"

"Thought you'd planned to continue taking the Prince's easy coin for service."

He laughed. "I did—and I do. I command the barrack outside Urfu. Hot and dry, the way a sensible man likes it, and enough leave and coin to let me hold the attentions of a merchant's pretty daughter in the City itself."

Liatt laughed in turn, gave the dog a shove as he interpreted that as permission to jump on her. "*Captain* Elegance, I'm suitably impressed! Well, yes, there is something you can do to aid me; this evening when we put ashore, and tomorrow night." She flipped her cloak aside, pulled the sword free. "Remember this? It's been living in a box for a few years. I'm fine, but the blade needs a lesson or so." And as Elgan goggled at her again, she swatted his hand, much as she'd clipped Kedru moments before. "Stop that. I don't doubt I could still gut you with it, but not with any style."

"Ah. Style." Elgan grinned. "What happened to the knives?" He stepped back a pace, and his companion stumbled back into the shed wall with a gasp as she slipped two from unseen sheaths. "Still have them, very—ah—very good, Liatt!"

"Only good in certain kinds of fights, I have the feeling I'll need the sword." Liatt sighed. "Don't give me a hard time, Elegance—yes or no? I'll pay, of course, whatever you—"

"Don't insult me," Elgan replied stiffly. "Pay be damned. I'll probably still learn things from you, woman, you're not fooling anyone! And so will my young friend here. Tonight after we tie up. And tomorrow. But on a ship that size, we'll be bound to see each other before then."

"No doubt. I'm running out of time, Ked and I have to go find food. Come on, Dog."

"Share with us, if you like."

"Hah. Still seasoning everything with those tiny little green and red peppers? I remember your idea of food, Elegance, and so does my poor burned stomach. I think I'd be better with my own." His laughter followed them down the docks.

They tied up the first evening an hour before sunset, at a small dock. One of the passengers left there, a boy dragging a young goat behind him.

Two women in the dark, serviceable blue of Elduran priestesses took his place; Liatt noticed with amusement that the ferryman stared after the younger of them rather wistfully, but had made no attempt to trade *them* passage for favors. *Be fair, Liatt; a poor grubby creature like that probably doesn't think there's any other way for him to bed a woman. And he didn't know what you were when he offered.*

The dock ran along the side of a deep-bedded creek that in spring and high summer would be swift and wide; now it was shallow and sluggish; the ship's boy took his buckets well upstream so the drinking water would not be salty. The captain settled down on the docks with his braziers and two low, wide jars of meat and vegetable cubes soaking in some kind of oil and spice broth. Liatt's stomach growled as the strode up the dock in Elgan's wake, and she found herself regretting that copper: the food she'd bargained for had cost her nearly as much and wouldn't taste as good as the kebabs smelled.

Kedru whined as she tied his lead to the end of the dock; she cuffed him once and he dropped to his belly. Looked up at her mournfully. "Shut. And stay put!" The silence wouldn't last long, but he wouldn't be able to take off, either.

He whimpered most of the time she and Elgan fenced, but she found it easy to ignore him then; nothing mattered but her sword and her opponent's, the ground they fought on, Elgan's eyes and the right shoulder that still warned half a short breath ahead when he intended to lunge. They quit only when it was getting dark, and even then only because Elgan finally broke through her guard and cut her sleeve. "Foul! I couldn't see you!" she shouted as she stepped back and let her blade fall.

Elgan laughed. "Foul! Not in a real fight—!"

Liatt snorted in exasperation. Her shoulders were stiffening, a headache in the offing unless she could get it settled with a few drops of Jahno's tincture. A backrub would help, but even Elgan, with his merchant's daughter, might misinterpret the request and she was too tired and grumpy to deal with that. "That wasn't in the rules when we started, real."

Elgan laughed. "Well, no, so it wasn't. You'll cut my sleeve next, and my arm with it. And I'm starved."

She was sore all over the next morning, grouchy because of it. Elgan had remembered her ways that much, though: he and those with him left her alone until after midday food. By evening tie-up, she'd worked out enough of the kinks to allow her to work with him again, and if she wasn't all the swordswoman she wanted to be— well, she never had been. And the sword protected her, she was certain of that now. Did that make her good enough to defeat a vindictive sorcerer and his cohorts? Time would tell. At least she had confidence, coming into Urfu.

She left Elgan and his cronies at the dockside after getting directions from him for the inn the girl in Virith had recommended, and for a stable where she could buy a desert-trained horse. The fact that she was acquainted with the City's garrison commander, that she could use his name, assured her she'd be able to sell the horse back on her return. She'd need to, in order to get back to Jahno.

Jahno. *Little green gods, Jahno.* The past days had been so replete with change, something constantly happening, new sights and sounds or old and familiar ones, that it might have been Jahno and the village that were ten years in her past. And yet, there was a small irritating sensation, like an unscratchable itch, or an aching tight muscle that wouldn't respond to massage. It was buried deep most of the time, under her bargaining and purchasing, arguing with the dog who dug himself flat in the middle of a busy street at his first sight of a dromedary and absolutely refused to budge, the sights and smells of old, familiar Urfu and the teasing scent of desert beyond that. *Jahno, by all that's holy to anyone, anywhere, I'd almost swear I missed you!*

On the advice of a merchant-woman, she left the dog's hairy coat alone but shaved his belly close. It was the wrong climate for a dog bred to withstand the forest winters, but he'd be no more uncomfortable than she; if she'd followed her first intentions, he'd have had sunstroke the first hour, out there. She bought herself a dark, serviceable byrnus, loose enough to fit comfortably over her leather jerkin and small tri-circled armor; bought, too, short breeches and sandals that left her legs comfortably bare under the byrnus. Sand trickled into the open shoes, but they were still considerably more comfortable than the thick boots. She left her heavier gear at the stable, as surety for the horse; in return, the stablemaster—a gambling acquaintance of Elgan's—let her rent the animal. An unusual bargain indeed, particularly in

Urfu, and one for which she'd have to thank Elgan.
*He'd better not have the means of thanks in
mind,* she thought grimly. Too many years in a
conservative village had given her a slightly shocked
outlook on what had once been commonplace to
her: Women with no other coin sometimes bargained with their bodies. Most men accepted that
without thinking the worse of them—and so, if
they were driven to such bargains, did the women.
Liatt had made such bargains herself, all too frequently. Somehow, with Jahno like an unscratchable
itch in the back of her mind, she couldn't put
herself to that test now, though the purchases
she made ran her supply of coin perilously low.

The map was a costly item, but absolutely es-
sential, for it showed the locations of wells and
flood-ravines. The garrison had nothing to do with
the northern desert, but one of Elgan's men assured her that while he did not know the map,
he'd vouch for its maker. She had to be content
with that.

It took her two days to ready, and she was
nervous, uncertain whether she was stalling. But
in truth, from now on, she was traveling blind.
"Out there somewhere"—out in the desert north
and a little west—that was a considerable expanse
of territory. And what she'd find there . . .

It took Kedru a while to adjust to the horse—
the dog didn't like the smell of the mare, the smell
of her gear, the smell of her blankets. Liatt wasn't
certain *she* liked the noticeable odor of camel that
clung to the embroidered and tasseled woolen pad,
but there wasn't anything to do about it but hope
the breeze held. The mare for her part was un-

used to having a dog so near her feet; fortunately, she had no active dislike of dogs. It had been too many years since Liatt had ridden much, and the beast she and Jahno owned was no war-horse. Neither was the mare, but she was good for distance along the road that led north from Urfu, despite heat, sun and wind.

She rode most of the day through sand and patches of gray, low grass or spiny ground cover. Now and again, there would be a bush or two—gray-green and spiny like the weeds, and now and again she could see faded willow-brush, sign of a gorge cut out by infrequent flash floods. It was hot but dry, and so bearable. They rested most of the afternoon in the shade of a slab of sandstone that reared well over their heads. Liatt climbed this late in the day, but could see nothing around them save more desert—and Urfu, looking draggled and small indeed behind them, a huddle of red-roofed, white-washed mud huts on the edge of the enormous Salten Sea.

It took her time to locate the landmarks that guided her to the first well—too long away from too many things, she thought, and reading a map one of them. It was nearly dark when she found the site, but the well was where it should have been, the water reasonably clear and cool. She moved a little away from the well and set her camp where a bramble thicket could shelter her and the animals from the worst of the wind and let her build a small cooking fire. That would be put out as soon as possible; she felt utterly exposed out here, and even though Kolos could find her no matter how well she hid, she didn't intend to give others any assistance. Whether they were looking for Liatt or just any traveler fool enough to be out here alone.

The horse accepted her canvas square of grain, rubbed against Liatt's hand when the woman gave her a bucket of water. "You're a love, aren't you?" Liatt murmured. Kedru nudged her leg and whimpered. "Shut, jealous dog. What did he call you— Gray? What kind of name is that for a sweetheart?" She ran the rough brushes across the mare's sweaty back and put her on a long lead so she could go roll in the sand before dark.

It got dark fast, after the sun went down—and quiet. So quiet all she could hear once the fire went out was the scree in her ears. When some insect began chirking nearby, she jumped and had her right hand on the ankle dagger before she realized what it was.

The dog's silence should have reassured her; but with *this* dog, she didn't feel certain she'd be forewarned of intruders. She slept uneasily and woke at first light feeling that she hadn't slept at all.

The uncertain road petered out before midday and left her to pick a way through thick brush and blowing sand. A broad overhang gave them shade for a noontime rest stop, but there was little grass for Gray and no water. Night camp wound up being less than an hour's travel from the rest stop; one of the marked wells was at that point, the next nearest too far to make before dark.

So far, Kolos was giving no sign, and that made her nervous. What if he intended to lead her into the dessert, draw her far from civilization and then simply strand her there? Somehow she didn't *think* that was his purpose, as it made no sense, but it lurked in the back of her mind, growing stronger as two more days passed with no indication that he had wanted her badly enough to send a demon to Jahno's barn to destroy her.

Noon of the third day found them in the midst of brush and rock and constant wind, with no shelter from the sun. Liatt rigged the thin second blanket to form a crude sunscreen, tying the corners from four of the tallest thornbushes she could find. It was tight quarters under the resulting cover; fortunately Gray and Kedru were getting used to each other, and Gray wandered in and out after she finished the short water ration. There wasn't much for her to eat. Kedru charged off into the bushes twice after some small animal or other, but even he finally flopped out in the shade and stayed there. Liatt dozed; it was too warm for proper sleep, and she was more worried than ever.

Near sunset, the hot breeze died away completely. Liatt considered this for some time; crawled out of the shelter to gaze all around them. She could see nothing but brush and more brush, fading into hazy distance. "Bah." She spat, crawled back under the blanket and retrieved her belt pouch. She brought out the wrapped cake of incense, flint, and tinder and sat cross-legged in the dirt for some moments, weighing alternatives. She knew better than to attempt to Build out on the desert. Wind made walking on the Way treacherous, even though it didn't much affect the Stair-building, and she really didn't feel like checking the quality of her virtue by trying it now. Then again—

"Damn everything. All right. I won't try to walk, I'll just climb. The Stairs are protected, I'll be safe if I stay on them. But I can't go much farther, I haven't supplies for much longer out and also back. Damn and damn again." She set a corner of the cake alight, bent down to sniff the thin line of smoke. Kedru slowly sank to his belly as she looked around, and she laughed light-headedly. "Stay put, dog. Guard Gray."

For some reason, it was difficult to concentrate on the first several steps, and the sun was ominously low by the time her feet were on a level with the roof of the shelter. Gray, grazing at the length of the tether, snorted nervously and backed away from the strange sight of human feet at nose height. Liatt grinned and went back to work on another step.

After the seventh, the rest of the stair came quickly. She stood on the twentieth, gazing around her. There wasn't time for much of a look, with the sun so low. Unfortunately there wasn't much to look at, either. South, she could barely make out the faintest silver that marked the inland sea, and Urfu was not visible at all. East and north the desert shaded off into brush and more brush, with not even rock or a hill to break the desolation. Due west it was nearly impossible to see for the level rays of the setting sun. Northwest, though: there were mountains there, perhaps a day's travel. More, likely, she thought gloomily. Distances here were deceiving indeed. Just this side of the mountains, partially shrouded in shadow, she thought perhaps there might be something else: towers, possibly. Something caught light and gave it back dazzling red, as though sun had touched on a window, high up. She edged back and forth on the step, but could make nothing of it.

"Well—try again in the morning, I suppose. I suspect we'd better get moving if we want water tonight, though. *Damn, what is that?*" She held a hand against the left side of her face and unwittingly took a step forward.

The result was instantaneous and catastrophic. A wild gust of wind caught her like a rootless weed and blew her head over heels across the Way, sending her hurtling northward, toward the curiosity she'd seen just short of the mountains.

It didn't hurt, being bowled across the sky; it was frightening, but she was more worried abut her daggers than the uncertainty of rolling along at a tremendous clip well above the ground. One or two of the sheaths weren't that well sewn at the tips, she could wind up cut to ribbons if she couldn't manage to stop, soon. And every moment took her farther from her horse, her dog, food and blankets.

And—surely—nearer to Kolos.

The ride ended abruptly; she had one brief, dizzy glimpse of dark stone buildings before she began to fall. Whatever was below her was flat, near black, shining. She tried to tuck into a ball, tried not to think. Mercifully, she blanked out just before she landed, flat, on Kolos' inner court.

She couldn't have been unconscious for more than a moment or so; she lay still, fingers exploring the surface on which she found herself. The neck-sheath was digging into her back, but so far as she could tell, she hadn't hit hard: she could breathe, and nothing hurt. *Nothing hurts yet*, she amended grimly. *Give Kolos a chance.*

She opened her eyes to a dark blue sky, a circular view of buildings—and an inner circle, much nearer—of faces.

There were six of them, two with bows at the ready, another holding a spear. Three with swords. Kolos' inner guard, Kolos' pretty boys. His taste hadn't changed, from what she could see of them. She grinned. "I should be flattered, six of you to one winded old woman! Where is he?" Silence. She tried to sit up, but the spear came to rest against her armor and pushed her flat again. "Stop that!" she snapped, and swatted the pole aside. "You don't want me mad, do you? I want to sit up, and I want to talk to Kolos, so one of you sweet things go and fetch him for me!" The boy with the spear flushed.

"I was right; charming as ever. Let her up. She can count, she's not going to kill all of you." A rather resonant voice came from behind her. She sat, twisted around to sit cross-legged. The armsmen backed away, were gone.

"I have no reason to waste charm on you, wizard. You wanted me, I'm here. What now?"

"Sorcerer, not wizard. Well . . . perhaps a cup of wine—"

"What, wine and poison? That was always a favorite of yours wasn't it?"

Kolos sighed elaborately. Spread his hands wide. "You used to have brains, Nobly Born. If I had wanted you dead, I could have sent a demon intended to kill. Instead of one to warn."

"All right. So? Maybe you want the personal touch."

"Maybe." He sighed again. "I should, for all the trouble you put me to. And it truly, truly was not nice of you to kill that boy of mine—by Adda, I cannot even remember his name any more!— but I assure you, I was quite upset at the time."

"It was harder on the boy," Liatt replied dryly. And added with rising irritation, "Little green gods, can we go somewhere I can see you?"

For answer the sorcerer backed, turned and gestured her to follow. By this time, he was a pale garment in a darkly shadowed courtyard, nothing else. If his guards were about, she couldn't see them. She followed Kolos—now a half-shadowed figure in a long robe that might have been shades of blue—down a dimly lit hallway, through a door veiled in netting and through another swath of netting to a low table and cushions. One of his scantily clad boys brought a tray with wine and a neatly sliced loaf of fine-textured white bread, and at a gesture from his master left them. Liatt gazed after him appraisingly. Kolos laughed, bringing her attention back to him.

"You're not so pretty as you were, Nobly Born," he remarked unpleasantly. Liatt snorted, pulled both cups to her and examined them in the light of the oil lamp. She took one, poured wine in it and gestured for him to drink as she poured the second cup. Laughing, he did. "I could have poisoned it and taken the antidote beforehand, you know."

"You could have," she agreed, and drank. "I was merely taking common sense precautions. You're not so pretty as you were, either, wizard—excuse me, sorcerer. Which wasn't much to begin with. Your taste is still good, though." He laughed, leaned into the light to take a piece of the bread, which he broke into small, dainty pieces. He laughed again as she waited with visible patience for him to eat first.

No, he wasn't attractive; never had been, but the years which had merely added a few lines, a few gray hairs and a few pounds to her—had been disastrous for him: his eyes were haggard, and heavy lines ran from both sides of his nose into his jawline. He'd gone heavy, added jowls, and his hands—once the nicest thing about him, deft slender fingers and capable palms—were pudgy and soft.

"Your own taste is still good, then? One frankly wondered, my dear—a peasant like that!"

"There's nothing wrong with Jahno," she snapped.

"You would know better than I. But for a Duke's daughter—"

"Kolos," she interrupted tiredly. "If you are attempting to anger me, you are certainly going about it in the right way. I am not a Duke's daughter! I am not to be addressed as 'nobly born.' Understand? My father—may he rot forever—is seventeen years dead, and I disowned him in the same breath he disowned me. And you didn't go to all this trouble just to get yourself a Sin-Duchessina here, did you?" Still grinning maliciously, Kolos shook his head. "Well then," she continued, "I happen to be a busy woman, and I also happen to have left a halfway decent dog and a thoroughly decent horse out where your wind caught me up. I'd like to get back to them, AND to my life—"

"—so you can rot happily ever after," Kolos interrupted flatly.

"I don't see it that way, thank you," she replied stiffly. "If you don't intend to kill me for Pedry—

that was your pretty's name, by the way—or for the Shioh jewel, what *do* you want?"

"Ah." Kolos helped himself to more wine and bread and settled back against his pile of cushions. "How interesting you should mention the jewel. Because—"

"It's not yours, damn you, and I refused to get it for you once. I haven't changed my mind."

"You should. After you joined the Prince's legions, actually some time after you went to play peasant—the priestesses lost it again, you know."

"Gods." Liatt sighed heavily, drank. The wine was a light one, well mixed with chilled water, and the bread was delicious: *How long since I've had decent wine or bread made with properly ground white flour?*

"They brought it out for a somewhat public ritual—and of course the Prelatery was ready for *that*. They've had it ever since."

"And you've been waiting, all this time—"

Kolos shrugged. "Well, no. I wanted it, of course. But there wasn't any worry about time, was there? Not for me. And the Prelatery had taken it and buried it deep in their underground trove. So long as they made no attempt to use it, it didn't seem worth the risk to go after it. After all, Nob—ah, dear Liatt, you were one of the best, and it wasn't sense to hire someone lesser. And you were—"

"I was furious," Liatt broke in flatly. "I still am. Keep that in mind."

"I shall try to. But you are also older, and that makes a difference. Ten years ago, if I had brought you here and tried to put to you a new bargain concerning the jewel, would you have been con-

tent to continue drinking my wine, eating my
bread, and listening to what I had to say?" He
laughed as she stared at him. "Of course not! But
now—however angry you may be, you *are* listening."

"I will not get the Shioh jewel for you, Kolos.
Whatever the alternatives are."

"I don't want it particularly." That did stop her.
She set her cup aside, let the bread fall unnoticed
to the table before her, and stared at him. "I
cannot manage it—well, look at me! Can you not
see?"

"Something went against you, didn't it?"

"Something I attempted, a while back," he admitted, rather unwillingly. "The jewel, here, would
drain what is left of my strength. Obviously, I do
not want that. I want you to take the stone—to
steal it from the Prelatery—and to find it a safe
hiding place. The priestesses may have the original claim to it, but they have no sense at all. Last
time, only the stone was taken. Next time, it may
cost Shioh priestesses, walls and all. Believe or
not, as you choose, but I would prefer that not
happen."

"I don't believe you, but that's not important.
Go on."

"I do not bother with the ordinary gods, but
Shia—I respect her. Mind, I'd have stolen her jewel
and taken what I needed from it. But I would not
actively contribute to the destruction of her House."
He sighed. "You are right. It isn't important, not
between you and me. Do what you want with the
jewel, when you have stolen it, just find it a safe
place. Later, perhaps, I will be able to convince
you to sell it to me, eh?"

"So far, you haven't convinced me to steal it. I

doubt you can." In a sudden access of rage, she slammed the cup to the table. "Little green gods, Kolos, *look* at me! I can't just take off on some fool's quest, not at my age!"

"Why not?" he demanded amiably. "You still like coin, don't you? And gems? Gold? You can still take care of yourself, I've seen that. Why do you think I let you come here?"

"Kolos—" she shook her head. He poured out the last of the wine, handed her more bread. Another of his boys came in with dates and fresh grapes. She was silent a while, ate and drank. Gods, it was like putting *hjasha* in front of an addict, what he was doing! And gods help her, he knew it! To go questing again, to ride through new lands, to sleep every night in a different place— she'd buried it so long, it rose now in a choking wave, threatening to overwhelm her.

And Jahno? Jahno, who'd left his small village so reluctantly to fight for his Prince, who'd been miserable away from his woods and his home, who'd returned to all of that so happily? Ten years later, it was as though he'd never left it: indeed, it had been that way mere days after he'd returned home.

Choices. She looked up as the boy who'd threatened her with his spear came forward with another pitcher of wine and another of chilled water. He flushed as he met her eyes, looked away, left quickly when Kolos gave him permission. Some people—like that boy, who'd been bought and paid for, who was now the sorcerer's property—some people had no choices, save a choice between compliance with a bad fate or death. Likely that one, given real choice, would by now have a woman and children.

She'd had only the choice between bad or worse once, and swore then she'd never be in such a position again. And now—freedom or Jahno? *It's not simple like that—it isn't that!* She felt guilty, embarrassed, even thinking of it that way. She wouldn't trade Jahno for anything, for anyone; he was important to her! But what went with him: Madda, the farm, the village, the hemmed-in, narrow life. Jahno wouldn't adjust; she'd have to. Choice . . .

"I can't do it," she said finally; her voice was high, strangled, and hardly sounded like hers at all.

"Can't!" Kolos raised his brows. "It's not a forever thing, my dear, just one simple errand, and coin to set you up in style, back in your peasant holdings."

"It's not that, and you know it!" she snarled at him. "One simple errand! I took change in stride years ago; I'm too old to do that now!"

"You're not even half my age," he said mildly. He sighed then. "Well, if you won't, you won't. I'll send you back to your beasts, you can go back to your woods and grow old with the rest of the peasants."

"Damn you—!" But it was hopeless, and she knew it. It pulled at her, dragged at her; damn Kolos and damn her alike, she wanted it! She could have gone years, could have gone the rest of her life not realizing how near the surface that desire lay, and now she'd have to work hard to bury it again. Poor Jahno, she wouldn't dare let him see how near she'd come.

"Take the fruit with you," Kolos said as he levered himself to his feet. "And I'll see you have water to take back."

Liatt held out a hand. Kolos looked at her in surprise, but took it. "You've done one thing for me—sorcerer. You've erased a bad taste from my mouth. I'm glad we met again under better circumstance."

"Better for *you*," Kolos replied dryly. "Go then. I won't bother you any more."

"Oath on that?" she demanded. He laughed.

"One *you'd* trust? Of course not! There's no such thing, is there?"

"Probably not." She watched him walk away, took the bundles from one of the boys: a good-sized jug of water to weigh down her shoulder, its strap both wide and padded to spread the heft of it. A belt-bag nearly as heavy, from which came the sweet smell of crisp grapes. At the boy's gesture, she turned and followed him back down the hallway, back into the courtyard.

It was totally dark now, the only light the stars. She glanced around, perplexed, wondering what she should do next; Kolos' spell wrapped around her and set her, in less than a startled breath, within touching distance of the blanket shelter she'd made that noon.

Gray shied nervously, and Kedru barked wildly until he recognized her scent. Liatt built up a fire, fed and watered them both, and lay back under the blanket, staring up but not seeing anything. It was a long time before she slept.

Three days steady riding brought her back to Urfu. She led Gray to the top of a low rise overlooking the barrack and the town. She sat there for almost an hour, gazing down at the red tiled roofs and the sea beyond. Across the water, she could barely make out the dark line of trees that marked the forest and her destination. As she watched, a ferry—possibly *Tradewind*—put in at port.

"End of it, horse," she murmured. Gray nuzzled the top of her head sympathetically, she would have sworn. "You go back to your stables here, and I go back to—ah, well. I knew I'd have to sooner or later." She pulled out the leather belt-bag that still held a little bread and fruit, and something else that had caught her eye the morning before—something she'd half expected when Kolos gave up so easily on trying to sway her, back within his walls. A small, thin square of hardened clay in a thinner clay wrapper: Kolos having the final word: "Should you change your mind, this is on account. If not, leave the bag at the Stone and Cup Inn, it will find its way back to me. I have no doubts of you, Nobly Born." A search of the bag divulged two gold coins, twenty-five silver, and three deep-red rubies set in a bronze pendant that hung from a heavy silver chain. Rubies had always been her favorite stones; somehow, he had known that. *Bribery. Flattery.* Oddly, she couldn't put the anger into that thought she knew she ought.

Well, she'd have to leave them once she returned the mare. Too bad: the pendant looked fine against her throat and it had a nice feel. And that much coin—she hadn't made that much altogether in all the years of breeding and selling calves and pups. "Never needed that much either, Liatt; leave be," she grumbled. She stood, stretched. The dog came to her side, sat and quietly waited. "Good," she said. His tail thumped once, but he no longer tried to jump on her. "Come." She took hold of

Gray's reins and started down the last stretch of road for Urfu.

Someone was riding toward her, coming up the hill at a goodly clip. Bags and packs hung from his saddle. He stopped as she came near. "Li!"

She stopped. Stared as he dropped to the road and ran up to her. "Juh—Jahno?" It *was* Jahno, in dusty leathers, his ugly, ancient and broad-brimmed hat on his head, his severely plain sword banging against his leg. Half a dozen spears poked out of the pocket on the saddle and stuck up above the horse's head. "What are you doing here?"

"What do you think?" he demanded. "I came to help. Look," he added. He pulled a pouch from his jerkin, poured the contents into his other hand. Coin, silver and copper, mounded there. He carefully funneled it back into the pouch, knelt to pick up the pieces that fell to the road. "Some of that is yours, of course. Estia's calves, I got your price for them. The lady herself went for two silver."

"Jahno, you—"

"—sold out." He looked up at her. "Came after you."

"Jahno. Gods." She dropped onto one knee, gripped his shoulder. "I was coming back, you know."

"Oh—*I* know." He said it so confidently; but she knew better. "But not happily, were you? Shh," he added gently, and laid a hand against her lips when she would have protested. "I know, don't lie. We don't have to go back. I wasn't happy without you. Never realized how much the outside world had changed me, I was so happy to be out of the Prince's colors and home again. With you it was bearable—the village, my brother,

235

Madda, all of it. Without—well, never mind. Doesn't matter. We're out, now."

"Jahno, you can't just throw over your *entire life* like that!" she protested weakly. "You're as old as I am! What are we supposed to do?"

He shrugged, grinned like a boy. "Whatever we want, Li. Anything. We have the choice, haven't we?"

"Choice—" She let her head fall back and laughed, sitting in the middle of the dusty road. "Gods, Jahno! We do, don't we?"

"Well, we'll have to be a little careful, at first," he said as he pulled her to her feet. "It's more coin than I've seen in a long time, but it won't carry us far, you know."

"Won't have to," she said as she swung up onto Gray's back. She pulled out Kolos' pouch and tossed it to him; his eyes widened in surprise at the heft of it. "I was going to turn down this job; now it's ours, if you want it."

"Want it? What is it? What's this for?"

"Tell you later. Minor commission, a small task and a lot of coin payment. How'd you like to visit sunny Kalinosa?"

Jahno tossed the pouch back. "Never did get to see Kalinosa. We taking that dog?"

"The dog goes with us," Liatt replied firmly. "Let's go find me some food that isn't full of sand, and a real bath."

DAW

Savor the magic, the special wonder of the worlds of
Jennifer Roberson

THE NOVELS OF TIGER AND DEL

☐ SWORD-DANCER   (UE2152—$3.50)
Tiger and Del, he a Sword-Dancer of the South, she of the
North, each a master of secret sword-magic. Together, they
would challenge wizards' spells and other deadly perils on a
desert quest to rescue Del's kidnapped brother.

☐ SWORD-SINGER   (UE2295—$3.95)
Outlawed for slaying her own sword master, Del must return to
the Place of Swords to stand in sword-dancer combat and
either clear her name or meet her doom. But behind Tiger and
Del stalks an unseen enemy, intent on stealing the very heart
and soul of their sword-magic!

CHRONICLES OF THE CHEYSULI

This superb fantasy series about a race of warriors gifted with
the ability to assume animal shapes at will presents the Cheysuli,
fated to answer the call of magic in their blood, fulfilling an
ancient prophecy which could spell salvation or ruin.

☐ SHAPECHANGERS: BOOK 1   (UE2140—$2.95)
☐ THE SONG OF HOMANA: BOOK 2   (UE2317—$3.95)
☐ LEGACY OF THE SWORD: BOOK 3   (UE2316—$3.95)
☐ TRACK OF THE WHITE WOLF: BOOK 4   (UE2193—$3.50)
☐ A PRIDE OF PRINCES: BOOK 5   (UE2261—$3.95)

DAW